THE DRAGONFLY EFFECT

Look for more action and humor from
GORDON KORMAN

The Hypnotists series
The Hypnotists
Memory Maze

The Swindle series
Swindle
Zoobreak
Framed
Showoff
Hideout
Jackpot
Unleashed

The Titanic trilogy

The Kidnapped trilogy

The On the Run series

The Dive trilogy

The Everest trilogy

The Island trilogy

Radio Fifth Grade

The Toilet Paper Tigers

The Chicken Doesn't Skate

This Can't Be Happening at Macdonald Hall!

GORDON KORMAN

THE DRAGONFLY EFFECT

BOOK THREE OF THE HYPNOTISTS

SCHOLASTIC PRESS / NEW YORK

FOR HOWARD NEWMAN, PSY.D.
BEVERLY HILLS MIND-BENDER

1

The M1 tank rumbled across the Oklahoma countryside, its long gun sweeping back and forth on the rotating turret. The commander's eyes never left the screen. He had it on the highest authority — post rumor — that a lot of top officers would be watching this training exercise. The three members of the tank crew knew they had to be ready for anything.

The commander scanned the image of flat land and scrub brush, expecting the unexpected. When it happened, though, he was still caught completely off guard.

The tank's driver spotted it, too.

"Is that a *kid*?" he asked in disbelief.

The commander stared. The figure that had stepped out from behind a tree and was walking toward them at a leisurely pace looked like he had just gotten off a school bus. He was probably around twelve or thirteen, tall for his age and slender, with light brown hair. He was dressed in jeans and a T-shirt.

The commander was astounded. Was this some kind of trick? Were the generals throwing him a curveball to see how he'd react to a middle-school kid strolling out in front of a speeding tank?

"Stop!" the commander barked to the driver. "You're going to run him down. Stop!"

The corporal was already braking. The M1 rolled to a halt, and the kid stood before it in the shadow of the long gun.

The commander scrambled up the ladder to the hatch. "Be ready to get us out of here on my word!" he tossed down to his crew.

He popped the top and emerged, staring at the slight figure dwarfed by tons of military armor.

The kid took something out from behind his back. A weapon? No, it was a small electric megaphone. He brought it to his lips and spoke four words:

"Look into my eyes . . ."

The commander did. And what amazing eyes they were — large and luminous, a pale green that changed to blue, then darkened through indigo to a deep violet.

"You are very calm now . . . very relaxed . . ."

The commander was amazed to find that he *was* calm. In fact, he couldn't recall having ever felt quite so tranquil. He was still aware that he was in the middle of a major exercise, but that didn't seem so important anymore.

The boy spoke through the megaphone again. "Now you will order your crew to unload all your ammunition. Toss it on the grass beside the tank."

By the time the Humvee roared up, heavy tank shells were scattered like ten pins on the grass all around the M1.

An irate military officer jumped out of the Humvee. His name was Colonel Roderick Brassmeyer, and he was the director of the army's Hypnotic Warfare Research Department, also known as HoWaRD.

Brassmeyer was crimson with rage. "What's going on here?"

Twelve-year-old Jackson Opus faced down the colonel's anger, but kept his eyes averted. "I disarmed the tank."

"You weren't supposed to disarm the tank!" Brassmeyer roared. "Your orders were to instruct the commander to fire on Building F!"

"I decided this was safer," Jax explained.

"You don't decide! *I* decide! You follow orders!"

"Yeah, but what if there's somebody in there?" asked Jax.

"There's nobody in there! It's a target! You've ruined the whole maneuver!" He looked up at the tank commander, who had resumed his place atop the turret. "Lieutenant, restore this ordnance!"

The tank commander wouldn't even glance in Brassmeyer's direction. His eyes remained on Jax.

"Oh, sorry, I haven't broken the mesmeric link yet." Jax turned to the commander. "When I snap my fingers, you'll awake feeling refreshed and happy —"

"Not too happy," the colonel interjected in an irritated tone.

"— and you'll do everything Colonel Brassmeyer tells you to do."

"You don't need that last part," Brassmeyer growled. "He's a soldier. *He* knows how to follow orders."

Jax snapped. The commander seemed startled for an instant, then saluted his superior officer.

"Sir!" he called out. Spying the scattered ammunition, he added, "Uh — what just happened, sir?"

The colonel swallowed an angry retort and softened. "Don't worry about it. You were just following orders — which is more than I can say for this young civilian here."

Brassmeyer had been in the US Army for thirty-five years. He'd seen action on three different continents, and had trained with every conceivable piece of equipment. But *this* weapons system — the one he was now in charge of developing — had to be the most bizarre.

Hypnotism.

2

The first thing Jax had learned about the Hypnotic Warfare Research Department was that, technically, it didn't exist. The soldiers stationed at Fort Calhoun believed that the low warehouse in the northwest quadrant housed the post archives — endless shelves holding tens of thousands of boxes dating back to the 1920s.

In reality, the building was the headquarters of a top secret project centered around nine civilians of varying ages. They had only one thing in common: All were mind-benders.

It had come to the attention of the army that there were hypnotists out there — people who could command the obedience of others just by gazing into their eyes. The purpose of HoWaRD was to develop military uses for mesmeric power — from hypnotizing a tank commander to swaying the decisions of a world leader across a negotiating table.

A year earlier, Jackson Opus hadn't even known what a mind-bender was, much less realized that he was one. Yet Jax was much more than an ordinary hypnotist. He was the nexus of the two greatest bloodlines in mesmeric history — the Opus and Sparks families. Neither of his parents had any hypnotic power at all. But the two clans had come together in Jax, endowing him with the potential to be the most gifted mind-bender ever — "the real McTavish," as Axel Braintree had described it.

The thought of Axel brought a sharp stab to Jax's chest. Braintree had been Jax's mentor and the founder of the Sandman's Guild. If it hadn't been for Jax, the old man never would have left his comfortable, oddball life in New York.

And, Jax reflected ruefully, *he never would have died trying to protect me from Dr. Elias Mako.*

Mako was in jail now, but that was a small comfort. Axel was gone.

The Jeep dropped Jax off in front of the building. Captain Pedroia, HoWaRD's psychiatrist, was there to meet him at the door.

"How did it go?" Pedroia asked.

"Not so good," Jax answered. "The hypnotism part went okay, but I messed up following the rest of the orders."

Pedroia sighed. "You're a nice kid, and I know you've been through a lot. But you just don't understand the colonel. He's a hundred and ten percent army, real spit and polish. He can only operate one way — his way. He tells you what to do, and you do it."

"Sometimes I'm tempted to bend the guy just to mellow him out," Jax admitted.

"Don't ever say that, even as a joke!" the psychiatrist snapped. "The army may be the greatest fighting force the world has ever known. But make no mistake — they're scared of what you can do. If they get the slightest sense that you might turn against them, they'll lock you up and throw away the key. *I* know you're only kidding. The colonel, though? He has no sense of humor — as in zero."

On some level, Jax understood that he should be grateful to the military for the protection they were offering him and his family. When Colonel Brassmeyer had scooped him up from the streets of New York, Jax had been under attack by Dr. Mako and his Sentia Institute, under arrest by the NYPD, and devastated by the loss of Axel Braintree. At the time, the army was the only safe haven available. It had been the best of a selection of bad choices, which didn't change the fact that it was a bad choice. His parents had gone from having prosperous careers to no careers at all. Yes, the military was looking after them, but they were leading boring, purposeless lives. And though Jax had a purpose, it was the *army's* purpose, not his own.

Technically, he was free. He wasn't a soldier, and he wasn't under arrest. His official status was "under military protection." Yet it had never been made clear to him what that meant.

"This is really hard on my mom and dad," he told the doctor. "I'm wondering if maybe I should just quit."

Captain Pedroia turned pale. "That wouldn't be safe! We all know what happened in New York."

"Yeah, but Dr. Mako is in jail and Sentia has disbanded. Why do I still need protection?"

"This is a small world full of spies," the psychiatrist explained. "If the army found out about you, somebody else can find out about you, too. Do you think Dr. Mako's the only bad guy out there?"

Jax was taken aback. "You mean — we can't leave if we want to?"

"That's the wrong question," Pedroia replied carefully. "Why would you want to? You're safe here, and you're serving your country."

Jax stared at him in dismay. It came out okay the way Pedroia said it. But when you cut away all the trimmings, it sure sounded like Jax was a prisoner.

Another part of army life Jax wasn't too fond of was the food. HoWaRD's meals were sent in from the officer's mess, and *mess* was the right word for it. It wasn't horrible, exactly, but everything was cooked in such bulk that all the dishes tasted the same, including fish sticks, cheeseburgers, green beans, and fruit salad. The gravy was gray and covered practically everything, and the pizza was enough to turn a New Yorker's hair limestone white. Jax knew it was even worse for his parents, who had enjoyed fine Manhattan dining before all this craziness began.

The mind-benders of the Hypnotic Warfare Research Department ate in a small dining room off their main work area. Jax took his seat at the round table and looked down at his tray without enthusiasm. Chicken à la king with a side of asparagus spears — also known as library paste and soggy cigars.

"What's the matter, Dopus?" rumbled a deep, unfriendly voice. "Don't you like sludge?"

Jax didn't bother to look up. He and Wilson DeVries had been hypnos at Sentia together, and enemies from day one. Back then, Jax had been Dr. Mako's star, and Wilson had been Dr. Mako's thug. He was still a thug — fifteen years old and built like an NFL linebacker. Wilson loved Fort Calhoun, and not just because being chosen for HoWaRD was probably the only thing that had kept him out of juvie when Mako went to prison.

Sludge or not, Wilson pounded down a remarkable amount of the food here. He wore heavy GI boots, even though the HoWaRDs weren't required to. If he could have gotten away with it, he would have asked the army to outfit him from head to toe. It went with his tough-guy image.

Wilson's divorced parents lived in New York and St. Louis, so he was here on his own, quartered with the other male HoWaRDs. To him, this was all a big adventure — or at least sleepaway camp for hypnotists.

"Can it, Wilson," ordered Evelyn Lolis, who was in her thirties, as tall as Wilson, and not easily intimidated. She had been a member of Axel Braintree's Sandman's Guild — although she'd spent most of her energy lobbying to change the name to Sand*person's* Guild. "Lay off Jax. Brassmeyer's leaning on him, and we all know what that's like."

"That's old news," Wilson scoffed. "I took down a CIA agent in the exercise today. The guy's trained to resist torture, but I bent him just like *that*." He snapped his fingers for emphasis.

"Get over yourself, sonny," advised Eunice Krieder, who could easily have been the boys' grandmother. "We've all bent CIA agents. It's nothing special." Eunice had raised eleven children, using generous doses of mesmeric power. Until the army had come to recruit her, she hadn't realized that her ability was anything more than positive parenting.

"The colonel decides what's special, and what isn't," Wilson muttered. "He was pretty impressed."

"A spy isn't harder to hypnotize than anybody else," Jax commented. "Some subjects have more natural resistance than others, but it has nothing to do with CIA training."

"Like you know anything about it!" Wilson shot back. "It's all over HoWaRD that you botched the tank maneuver today. Way to earn your name, Dopus!"

Jax lifted his head and peered deliberately into Wilson's face. The bigger boy almost dislocated both shoulders turning away. Wilson was a pretty good mind-bender, but his ability could not begin to match the force of Jax's color-changing eyes. Even experts like Dr. Mako and Axel Braintree could only begin to guess how strong Jax might become. There were nine recruits in HoWaRD, but it was clear that the entire program had been designed around Jax. At least, it had been word of his abilities and achievements that had prompted the government to investigate whether hypnotism could be put to military use.

Suddenly, Jax was aware of an odd sensation, almost like swallowing water down the wrong pipe — but in his mind rather than his throat. He had long since learned to recognize when someone was trying to hypnotize him — a stirring in the brain that oozed along his spine.

He looked across the table at the youngest member of the HoWaRD team — a short, slight boy with fair crew-cut hair and a seemingly permanent sniffle. Eight-year-old Stanley X was a ward of the United States military. He had been discovered in an orphanage in Houston, where the staff had suspected that something strange and paranormal was taking place between him and the other orphans. At HoWaRD, the boy was only beginning to discover his mesmeric gifts.

Stanley's huge eyes, almost yellow gold, gave him an owl-like appearance, which was magnified by his slight features. Of the nine HoWaRDs, Stanley was the least experienced in the art of hypnotism. He was already a powerful mind-bender, but like most eight-year-olds, he was distractible, and struggled to keep a subject under mesmeric control. He was a source of constant frustration to Brassmeyer — the boy had so much potential but so little maturity. To Eunice, who had raised kids, Stanley was a typical eight-year-old; to the colonel, he was the equivalent of a piece of equipment that wouldn't perform the way it was designed to.

Yet, for all his shortcomings, Stanley was the only member of the HoWaRD team who could reach out with his mind and touch Jackson Opus. Jax suspected that it wasn't even on purpose. That was the unnerving part. If the kid was this strong without even knowing what he was doing, what would he be like when he was a little older and had learned to direct all this energy?

Jax turned his luminous eyes on Stanley and fired his own hypnotic potshot back at the eight-year-old. Stanley recoiled, but not as much as Jax expected him to.

"Leave Wilson alone," Stanley said resentfully.

This was another sore point. Wilson treated Stanley like a cockroach who'd taught himself to stand upright. Stanley responded by hero-worshipping Wilson. It made sense in a way. Wilson was everything Stanley wasn't — older, bigger, stronger, tougher.

Wilson grinned at Jax. "Yeah, Dopus. Lay off."

"I'm at the end of my rope with you two!" exclaimed Eunice in exasperation.

A burst of rapid-fire Romanian came from Anatoly Cescu, another HoWaRD. It effectively quieted the table, since nobody else spoke Romanian. Although Anatoly was a gifted mind-bender, his English was so limited that he had to perform hypnotism with an interpreter at his side. Even then the language barrier could be tricky — like the exercise in which Anatoly's mesmeric command to reveal secrets had been translated as "Spill your guts!" and his subject had vomited all over the interrogation room. Still, the army remained committed to Cescu's training, since true military hypnotism would have to account for different cultures and tongues.

There were three other HoWaRDs. Across from Jax sat Jerry Katsakis, a recent college grad who had been working in the complaint department of Marshall Field's department store in Chicago. The army had discovered him because his client satisfaction rating was 100 percent — a number that would not be possible without some kind of mesmeric influence on his customers.

Dirk Starkman was the former head of the West Coast branch of the Sandman's Guild, and had volunteered for HoWaRD after the death of Axel Braintree. The Guild was a support group for mind-benders who were struggling to resist the temptation to use their mesmeric gifts for personal gain. But while the New York branch consisted of con artists and pickpockets, the Los Angeles Sandmen were mostly unemployed actors trying to kick the habit of hypnotizing producers and casting directors into hiring them.

"I was an aspiring actor once, too," the stocky Dirk had confessed. "I bent this director to cast me as Robin Hood. The problem was, I weighed over three hundred pounds, and I had to wear those skinny green tights! You know how they talk about how much movies gross? Well, my movie was *truly* gross. That's how the West Coast chapter of the Guild got started."

The final chair around the table was occupied by Ray Finklemeyer. Ray used to make his living as the Amazing Ramolo, a stage hypnotist who specialized in school groups. It had been Ray who'd first discovered Jax and recommended him to Elias Mako.

Jax was never completely at ease around Ray because the man had once worked for Sentia. The army seemed to trust him, though.

But that didn't mean much, because Jax didn't trust the army.

3

As bad as the food was, Jax always gulped it down quickly so he could enjoy a few minutes to himself before the afternoon's activities began. Brassmeyer had an endless to-do list: The HoWaRDs bent soldiers to make them give up their weapons, give up intelligence, and just plain give up. The HoWaRDs even bent one another, trying to learn who had resistance to whom, and for what reason. They worked with volunteers to see if hypnotism could be taught to ordinary people. This last effort was a pet project of the colonel's. Brassmeyer dreamed of an entire division of GI mind-benders marching into hostile territory and conquering the enemy without firing a single shot. But Jax knew it wasn't going to happen. Although hypnotic power could be developed and refined, it couldn't be created out of nothing. Which didn't stop Brassmeyer from trying to force it to happen.

"Nobody likes a smart aleck, Opus," the colonel told him when Jax had the nerve to complain about all the hours watching soldiers staring at each other.

"But it's never going to work," Jax persisted. "It's a total waste of time!"

"I *own* your time," Brassmeyer informed him smugly. "That makes it *my* time. And I'll waste it any way I want to."

That day, when Jax, Wilson, and Stanley went for their mandatory three hours of schooling, the first vocabulary word was:

insubordination *(n)*: disobedience to authority, especially in the military
   See also: *mutiny*

The instant Jax stepped out of the building, he felt his mood lighten a little. The walls were closing in on him in that place. It was getting worse every day. Here, he was still on Fort Calhoun property — living behind barbed wire. But at least a guy could breathe out in the open. Not having to look at Wilson helped.

The northwest quadrant was the quietest part of the post, but it was still a busy place. Soldiers and a few civilians walked here and there, and the occasional jogger went by on a circuit from the parade ground located to the south. There was car traffic, too — mostly Jeeps and Humvees. Fort Calhoun was a small city, offering fast-food restaurants, movie theaters, and grocery stores. There was everything — unless you were a lost New Yorker yearning for home.

A military police Jeep was heading Jax's way, the driver rubbernecking, as if searching for something. With a jolt of alarm, Jax recognized the two people under arrest in the backseat.

He broke into a run, and by the time he reached the vehicle, he was sprinting, flashing the Fort Calhoun ID that he always wore around his neck. "Mom! Dad! What's going on?"

Ashton Opus tried to put on a brave face. "It's just a misunderstanding. We went off post and forgot to bring our badges. It's not a crime."

"Actually, it is," the MP informed him. "Especially when you're looking at a secure installation with binoculars." He indicated two sets of field glasses on the front seat beside him.

"We were *bird-watching*!" Monica Opus exclaimed bitterly.

Bird-watching had been Captain Pedroia's suggestion. Jax had begged the psychiatrist for something to occupy his poor parents while their son was here at HoWaRD. There was quite literally nothing for them to do — and they were doing it. Mom was trying to keep herself occupied sprucing up their dreary military-issue quarters with decorative items ordered over the Internet, and Dad had become addicted to a new social networking and gaming site called FreeForAll. Ashton Opus was a cultured and educated man in his prime. When he looked back on this part of his life, he would see himself watching videos of other people's pets drinking out of the toilet.

The Opuses were nothing less than miserable here. True, it was impossible to die of boredom. But the black shadows under their eyes told of sleepless nights, and the lines etched into their faces could not be explained by worry alone.

Looking at them, handcuffed together in the backseat, Jax's heart was wrung. "Let them go! They're my parents!"

The MP was unimpressed. "Good. They're your parents. Who are you?"

Jax bit his lip. As far as the rest of Fort Calhoun knew, there was no such thing as the Hypnotic Warfare Research Department. The MP probably assumed he was a soldier's son from one of the family cottages.

"You have to talk to Colonel Brassmeyer," Jax advised. "He'll vouch for all three of us."

"Already tried that," the MP replied. "The colonel's off post for the rest of the day. I'll have to keep these two on ice until I can reach him."

"Don't say that!" Mr. Opus exclaimed. "Jax has an ID, and he's obviously our son — why would he claim to be if he wasn't? Can't we be sensible about this?"

"I have my orders," the MP informed him. "There's nothing anybody can do."

Jax knew that wasn't strictly true. He fixed the MP with a double-barreled stare. Almost immediately, a new image appeared in his field of vision. It looked very much like a picture-in-picture window on a TV — Jax, standing by the Jeep, staring straight ahead. It meant that a mesmeric link had been forged between Jax and the MP. He was inside the man's mind, peering back at himself, seeing what the soldier saw.

It meant the MP was under his power.

"I guess you're pretty tired," Jax said conversationally. "I think you should rest a bit. . . . That's it. . . . You're very relaxed. . . ."

"Oh, honey, this is not a good idea," Mrs. Opus began. "You know the rule."

The rule she was referring to came from Brassmeyer. It went something like: *If you ever hypnotize anyone without direct orders from me, I'll skin you alive and nail your hide to the nearest wall.*

But there was no way Jax was going to let his parents spend a day under arrest for the innocent offense of trying to make the best of a bad situation that the army had foisted on the Opus family in the first place.

Besides, a good mind-bender knew how to cover his tracks.

He held up a hand to quiet his mother and continued, "Now you will unlock the handcuffs, give back the binoculars, and let them come with me. When I snap my fingers, you'll wake up, feeling calm and refreshed. You never found two people with binoculars outside the post. You never saw them at all, and you never saw me."

The MP immediately released Mom and Dad. They were grateful to be free, but they couldn't hide their fascinated horror at this demonstration of their son's capabilities. Even Dad — who had grown up with hypnotic parents — would not meet Jax's gaze.

Jax snapped his fingers, and the man got back behind the wheel and drove off.

"Sorry, son," Mr. Opus said in a husky voice. "We didn't mean to put you on the spot like that. I hope it doesn't get back to the colonel."

"Don't worry, Dad," Jax assured him. "That MP's already forgotten us. It should be me apologizing to you guys. You're here because of me."

Monica Opus was distraught. "Don't ever blame yourself! You didn't ask for all this hocus-pocus! *We* gave it to you — our ancestors, anyway."

"This won't last forever, Mom and Dad. I promise we'll get our lives back. The minute Brassmeyer's through with me —"

"Don't make promises you can't keep," Ashton Opus interrupted. "Why would the army ever let you go? Look what you can do. Even the other hypnotists can't match your power."

"I don't know," Jax ventured, thinking of eight-year-old Stanley. "Maybe there's somebody coming up who can take my place."

He said it in a hopeful tone. But for some reason, the idea troubled him.

It was after three AM when Jax padded down the hall of their post cottage in search of a drink of water. As he passed the small living room, the glow of the TV caught his attention. It took him a moment in the dim light to spot his mother, sitting motionless in an armchair, staring blankly at the screen.

"Must be a good movie," he commented, keeping his voice low to avoid waking his father.

She was startled. "Huh — oh, this? I think it's an infomercial — that spray paint to cover up your bald spot. I just couldn't fall asleep tonight."

Tonight and every other night, Jax reflected morosely. And who could blame her? She used to be a chiropractor with a successful city practice — and now she was reduced to a faceless, purposeless life as a hypnotic fugitive and mother of the army's plaything.

Before he had a chance to think about what he was doing, he was staring into her careworn eyes, bringing all his mesmeric power to bear. It was a betrayal — no question about it. He had promised never to hypnotize his parents. This was in exchange for *their* promise to stop looking away every time he glanced in their direction.

But how could he let her suffer like this? And anyway, she wasn't going to remember what he was doing to her now.

Soon, the PIP image appeared — Jax's face as Mom was seeing it, peering down at her as she sat.

"You are feeling very sleepy. . . . Your eyelids are growing heavy. . . . All you can think about is your head hitting the pillow. . . ."

Almost immediately, his mother stretched and yawned.

"When I clap my hands, you'll go back to bed and fall into a deep, restful sleep. You'll wake up refreshed and you will remember nothing about seeing me tonight. And this is important — you'll feel happy and content."

He clapped once and watched as she started past him toward the master bedroom.

At least she'll get some sleep, he thought. The rest of his post-hypnotic suggestion was pretty much a lost cause. He'd learned from his two mentors — Mako, and later, Braintree — that this was one of hypnotism's few limitations.

It was impossible to command someone to be happy.

4

The F-15 cockpit was cramped, overloaded as it was with wires, hoses, buttons, switches, and dials. It all seemed to be swallowing the pilot in his flight suit — but that might have been the effect of the fish-eye lens that was broadcasting the video to Jax's monitor.

"You are very calm ... relaxed ... drowsy ..." Jax was saying into the microphone below his own camera.

"Not *too* drowsy," Colonel Brassmeyer murmured tensely from just over Jax's shoulder. "The last thing the air force needs is a drowsy fighter pilot."

"But you're not so drowsy that you can't fly the plane," Jax added quickly.

He could see himself now, eyes deep purple, through the mesmeric link — the picture-in-picture image of what the pilot saw. Jax's face was framed by a screen in the cockpit, surrounded by instruments. He was inside the man's mind.

This was the ability that made Jax unique, even among mind-benders. Most hypnotists needed to be face-to-face with their subjects. But Jax was so powerful that he could mesmerize remotely, via a screen. The implications were enormous, since a video clip could be broadcast on TV or distributed through the Internet to millions of viewers at the same time.

"Have you got him yet?" Brassmeyer urged. "Is he under?"

Jax waved him off with a gesture similar to swatting a fly. Remote hypnotism was not easy. Jax could do it, but it took all of his concentration.

The commander of the Hypnotic Warfare Research Department was not accustomed to being brushed off so dismissively. He opened his mouth to fire an angry rebuke, but Captain Pedroia stepped in and took the brunt of the colonel's anger.

"You have to let the kid be, sir," he counseled. "He can't keep the pilot under control and talk to you at the same time."

"The army has protocols!" Brassmeyer sputtered.

"He's not a soldier," the psychiatrist reminded him. "And there's nobody else in the world who can do what he's doing right now."

Jax maintained concentration on his monitor as the PIP image grew sharper and more vivid — his own face on the screen, the sky as the fighter jet knifed through it, the horizon, vague and distant. Along with the visual information, random details of the pilot's life began to leach through: He was twenty-four, from Ohio; he had a dog named Honus Wagger. There were also wisps of memory — a family Christmas; a high-school football triumph. The longer Jax spent inside the man's mind, the more he'd get of the true person.

Brassmeyer handed him a card with a list of instructions on it — mostly numbers representing speed, altitude, and heading. It meant nothing to Jax, but as he broadcast the commands to the pilot, he could see that the aircraft was executing a series of dramatic maneuvers. The earth replaced the sky and hurtled upward as the fighter went into a dive. This was followed by a barrel roll at such high speed that the world outside the cockpit was just a blur. The ground whizzed by as the pilot made an upside-down pass at low altitude. Jax could almost feel the F-15 shudder as it was put through its paces.

At last, he reached the final instruction on the card. "Initiate special order 4414."

The hypnotized pilot complied immediately. Through his peripheral vision, Jax could see Brassmeyer and Pedroia sitting forward in their chairs, watching breathlessly.

The plane was in another dive, the features on the ground growing larger every second. Jax waited for the pilot to pull out.

He didn't.

The fireball lasted only a split second before the video went blank.

Jax leaped to his feet and turned on Brassmeyer. "He *crashed*! He's dead! You made me kill him!"

"You're out of line, mister!"

"*You're* out of line!" Jax shot back. "The whole army's out of line if they think it's okay to waste somebody just for a stupid experiment! He was a *person*! He had a family — and a dog! Honus Wagger!"

The colonel was livid. "We're done here, Opus. Go someplace and cool off before I call the MPs."

"You won't get away with this!" Jax was in tears, but they were tears of rage. "I'm going to tell on you. I'll do it the army way. I'll find a general who can dump on a colonel the way you dump on everybody else!"

"Shut up, Jax," Pedroia said sharply. "Nobody's dead."

"He is! You saw!"

Brassmeyer regarded the captain disapprovingly. "We don't have to explain anything to this — brat!"

"You put me in charge of the mental health of the HoWaRD team," the psychiatrist argued. "If he thinks he caused that pilot's death, that's an unacceptable burden for a twelve-year-old to carry."

The colonel chewed this over, breathing hard. Finally, he turned to Jax. "Just this once," he fumed, "I'm going to explain to you what you've got no right to know. The pilot you bent was never in a plane. He never crashed."

"Don't tell me what I saw with my own eyes," Jax snapped back.

"You're making this very hard," Brassmeyer warned. "The pilot was in a simulator. We needed to see if a hypnotic command could bring down a plane. And you succeeded. But no one is dead. Honus Wagger still has a master."

"I saw fire," Jax persisted. But even as he said it, he picked up a faint impression of the picture-in-picture image through the pilot's eyes. Now he was pouring himself a cup of coffee. Dead people certainly didn't do that.

"The simulators are lifelike," Pedroia supplied. "And you saw what you thought was happening. Just because you're good with your mind doesn't mean it can't play tricks on you. Now why don't you quit while you're ahead? The colonel's been patient with you."

Jax studied his sneakers in embarrassment, yet stopped short of apologizing to Brassmeyer. Okay, this was just a simulation, but what about tomorrow? Why would the army have to practice bringing down a plane if they weren't prepared to do it for real one day?

Jax had already met someone who was willing to take mesmeric power to its catastrophic limit in order to achieve his goals.

His name was Elias Mako.

5

The Colston Maximum-Security Penitentiary in South Carolina was a grim place, with high walls of reinforced concrete ringed by multiple guard towers. It housed many of the most dangerous offenders in the prison system. Inmates were seldom seen in the common areas without handcuffs and leg-irons, surrounded by armed guards. It was a point of pride to the warden and his staff that no one had ever escaped from Colston in the facility's sixty-six-year history.

The cells were cramped and depressing, separated by two-foot-thick walls and iron bars. Comforts were virtually nonexistent beyond thin mattresses and skimpy blankets . . . except for isolation unit 1727 in cellblock D.

Compared to the other cells, it was a five-star-hotel suite. It was roomy, with a memory-foam bed and a sixty-inch wall-mounted TV offering four hundred seventy-five satellite channels. There was a computer and a well-stocked library. The furniture had been shipped from Harrods in London, and was made from the finest leather. Meals were delivered from local restaurants — not exactly gourmet, but infinitely better than prison food.

Most amazing of all, when the guards looked into isolation unit 1727, they noticed none of this luxury. They saw an ordinary cell with an ordinary inmate in an ordinary orange jumpsuit. There was nothing wrong with their vision. A powerful post-hypnotic suggestion was affecting their minds. They saw only what the inmate wanted them to see.

Life here was so comfortable that sometimes Dr. Elias Mako wondered why he would ever consider leaving. It was restful to stay in here and let the country forget the nasty business of his arrest and trial, and the fact that he'd been declared a menace to society.

But Dr. Mako had big plans — plans that could not be executed from inside Colston's massive walls.

The guard arrived with a tray from Barbie's Q. Excellent ribs, but the Styrofoam and aluminum foil definitely detracted from the dining experience. No matter. Dr. Mako wasn't planning to eat it anyway.

He peered into the guard's eyes and said, "Hello, Ralph. You will now come in and shut the door behind you."

Three minutes later, Ralph was wearing the orange jumpsuit and enjoying Barbie's ribs while Mako, in Ralph's uniform, was striding purposefully down the corridor.

His face did not match the picture on Ralph's ID badge, but that was not a real problem. It was the work of just a few seconds for Mako to hypnotize the sentries at the various checkpoints. Soon he was out of lockup altogether, enjoying a cup of coffee in the guards' break room. He exchanged a few pleasantries with the tall fellow who was restocking the snack machines. Several minutes later, it was Mako in the snack-machine man's coveralls, driving toward Colston's main gate in the vending company's van.

"That was fast," commented the sentry in the guardhouse.

"Have a 3 Musketeers," Mako offered, handing a candy bar up through the window.

It was an error. As the man moved to accept the gift, another sentry behind him got a good look at the van's driver — the single black brow, striking dark eyes, and hawklike Roman nose. It was not an appearance anyone would forget.

"Hey — you're not the same guy who came in here!"

Mako knew a moment of alarm. It would be easy to bend either guard, but not both at the same time.

His burning eyes brought the first sentry under his control in a matter of seconds. "Your partner is an escaping inmate. Arrest him before he gets away!"

And while the two guards wrestled on the floor of the booth, Mako reached in the door, pulled the lever that opened the gate, and drove out of prison forever. He was a free man.

There was much to be done.

6

Jax took his seat across from Dirk Starkman.

"Maybe I should just ring the bell right now and save myself the trouble," the former president of the West Coast branch of the Sandman's Guild announced in a good-natured tone.

Captain Pedroia was patient. "You know the colonel doesn't take shortcuts."

"I'm a little outgunned," the big man said plaintively. "If this was a pie-eating contest, on the other hand . . ."

Jax turned the full brunt of his color-changing eyes on Starkman's pudgy features. He felt a bit of a counterattack from his subject, but nothing to cause him any difficulty. Starkman was a protégé of Axel Braintree, but his actual powers were mediocre. Barely thirty seconds had gone by before Jax saw the PIP image appear.

"You are very calm," he intoned. "Very relaxed . . ."

The impressions seeped through the mesmeric connection — a lifetime of crash diets and exercise regimens, summer camps for overweight kids. Eventually the portly actor had become so sick of always being cast as the fat guy that he'd begun to use hypnotism to get better parts. Braintree had seen him on Broadway, playing Romeo opposite a Juliet who was a third his weight. Axel had known instantly that no three-hundred-pound actor could win that role except through hypnotism.

The presence of Braintree — even in someone else's thoughts — brought Jax enormous sadness.

"There are innocent children in trouble," he informed his subject, anxious to end the connection. "There's only one way to help them. You have to ring that bell. The quicker you get there, the sooner they'll be saved. Now wake up and *go!*"

Dirk Starkman had never moved so fast in his life. Even when he stumbled over a chair, his big legs kept pumping. He hit the ringer so hard that he knocked it off the wall.

He was still slapping at the spot where the bell used to be when he came back to himself, and assumed a sheepish grin. "I guess I lost."

"Big-time," Evelyn Lolis confirmed.

"Took you long enough, Dopus," Wilson spat. "Thought you were supposed to be special."

Jax didn't respond. The images of Braintree had left him shaken, and he didn't trust his own voice.

"Since you're so confident, Wilson," Pedroia jumped in, restoring the ringer to its place on the wall, "why don't you take Dirk's spot opposite Jax?"

"Sure," Wilson blustered, sitting down. "I'm not afraid of him."

Jax set his jaw, determined to get this over with. The

last thing he wanted was to spend too much time inside the head of this jerk.

Their eyes locked and Jax overpowered Wilson easily, bringing up a PIP image that was instant and vivid. Jax had already abandoned the notion of trying to convince Wilson to help children in trouble. Wilson didn't care about children or anybody else. He cared about Wilson, and that was as far as it went. Jax was about to issue a direct command when the wave of emotion hit him. There was no mistaking it: *hatred*. It was so angry and so raw that, for a moment, he looked away and almost lost the mesmeric link. This wasn't a clash of power against power. It was pure loathing and jealousy and ugliness — the kind of passion that Dr. Mako was an expert at recognizing and turning to his advantage.

"Wilson!" Although the encounter was silent, Jax was shouting, as if trying to make himself heard over a roar. "Ring the bell! Do it now!"

Wilson slouched over to the wall, rang the bell, and cursed under his breath at the knowledge that Jax had bested him yet again.

"I wasn't ready," he mumbled.

"Next victim!" chanted Starkman.

Jax was surprised to find Stanley X settling into the seat opposite him. The eight-year-old had never looked younger, with his huge owl eyes and serious expression. A tiny droplet hung from the tip of his perpetually runny nose. Was this little kid really about to take on Jackson Opus?

Jax turned to the captain. "You're joking, right?"

"What's the matter, Dopus?" Wilson challenged. "Scared of an eight-year-old?"

"This comes straight from the colonel," Pedroia reported. "Everybody versus everybody else. Let's get it over with."

With a sigh, Jax focused his concentration on Stanley's remarkable amber eyes. They were large — almost anime large — and seemed to glow with an inner fire.

The beginnings of the PIP appeared right on schedule, only to wink out a moment later, to be replaced by the familiar stirring in Jax's brain. Stanley had fought off his incursion and was trying one of his own. For an eight-year-old who barely understood what it meant to be a mind-bender, he certainly seemed to have talent — even against Jax, who took down experienced hypnotists like Evelyn Lolis and Ray Finklemeyer without breaking a sweat.

Next came that mental sensation of swallowing water down the wrong pipe. Jax fought it off and bore down on Stanley, but after a few seconds the feeling was back again.

"Relax," the boy told him.

Jax was amazed to find that he *was* relaxed. In fact, he was *awesome* — calm and utterly at peace with —

"No!" he exclaimed suddenly, twisting away from Stanley's gaze.

"Whoa! Whoa!" Wilson crowed. "Is Jackson Dopus *losing*?"

"Of course not!" Jax exploded. "I just —"

He fell silent. Just because Wilson was a muscle-head didn't necessarily mean he was wrong. If Jax had to avert his eyes to avoid being bent, then he was losing.

Pedroia seemed to read his mind. "It's not a contest, Jax. We're all learning how this works. If you change the rules halfway through, we won't be able to trust the results of the experiment."

"My bad." Jax's heart was pounding. "I'll get it right this time."

By now, he and Stanley were the center of attention as they squared off across the tabletop.

Once again, Jax took on the amber eyes, trying to channel the combined force of centuries of Opus and Sparks mind-benders that had come together in him. Stanley peered back, his owl-like features earnest.

Doesn't he understand how huge this is? Jax wondered in his dismay. No one was a match for Jackson Opus — nobody except Mako, anyway. Even Axel Braintree had lost the ability to penetrate his pupil's defenses a few months into his training.

And now some third grader marches in here and —

When the attack came, it was no mere water-down-the-wrong-pipe sensation. It was a jackhammer boring directly into Jax's brain. For an instant, it was nothing short of unbearable.

"You feel wonderful . . ." Stanley's voice persisted.

"No!"

Then it was over and Jax was awash in a sense of happiness and well-being, just as the voice had guaranteed.

He trusted the voice 100 percent. It never occurred to Jax to question the fact that it seemed to belong to a young child. It had promised him this euphoria and it had delivered. It was *good*. As long as he did as it asked, everything would be wonderful.

Jax was on his feet now, crossing the room. He didn't question it; the voice wanted this, and that was enough for him. He was completely unaware of the many eyes on him as he reached for the bell.

Ding!

The sound brought Jax back to himself in the midst of a rousing round of applause. Wilson boosted Stanley onto his shoulders and carried him around the room, where he was showered with backslaps and high fives from hypnotists and soldiers alike.

"Good one, Stanley," Jax offered in a muted tone. "Congratulations."

"Thanks." The solemn boy wasn't smiling exactly, but he was clearly pleased at all the admiration he was getting.

"Looks like there's a new boss hog around here, Dopus!" Wilson sneered.

Jax was amazed by the intensity of his reaction. Why should he care that Stanley X hypnotized him one time? For starters, Jax had just grappled with Dirk and Wilson, so he was probably a little worn down. Besides, he'd been bent before. It was no big deal. And anyway, he should be thrilled that someone was coming along to take a bit of the pressure off him. What had being number one gotten him so far? It had turned him and his family into exiles, it had nearly gotten him killed more than once, and it had made him into someone else's puppet — first Mako's, and now the army's. Some gift! It was more like a curse! If Stanley was going to take that off his hands, then the little guy was the best friend Jax ever had!

I should be happy about this, Jax told himself, watching Wilson jog around the room, bearing Stanley on another victory lap.

So why did it make him feel so uneasy?

7

Dr. Pedroia's office was in a small corner of the HoWaRD building. All the hypnotists had regular sessions with the team's psychiatrist. Just as regular soldiers had to ensure their bodies were in shape, those who worked with their minds had to keep up their mental health. The army did not want unstable mind-benders.

"The last shrink I saw had a cushier office — no offense," Jax commented, surveying the drab government-issue furniture. "He was on Park Avenue, thirty-fifth floor."

"Why were you seeing a psychiatrist back then?" Pedroia inquired.

Jax shrugged. "Misunderstanding. I was bending people by mistake, and I thought the PIPs were hallucinations. My folks were convinced I was crazy. If only it could have been that simple."

The captain was confused. "But surely you knew. You're descended from two great hypnotic families."

Jax shook his head. "Mom had no clue. She'd never even heard the name Sparks until Axel told us. And my dad . . . let's just say he didn't have the happiest childhood. It's not easy to be the non-hypnotic kid of two big-time benders. Did he weed the vegetable garden because he wanted to, or was he given a little nudge of encouragement?"

Pedroia was skeptical. "Your grandparents mesmerized their own son?"

"The Opuses have been doing stuff like that for centuries. You think the Light Brigade wanted to charge into the valley of death? Some great-great-granduncle bent the bugler to play the charge instead of the retreat. Pretty much wherever you look in history, there was an Opus in the middle of it, rigging the game to make a quick buck, or mixing in just because they could."

The psychiatrist was fascinated. "And your mother's family?"

"The Sparkses were different," Jax replied. "They were, like, nobility, even royalty. To them it was an art, or at least entertainment. Baron Bartholemeus Sparks had a living art gallery of hypnotized volunteers impersonating ancient Greek statues. His younger brother invited four hundred people to a foxhunt, then bent half of them into chasing a chipmunk while the other half watched. But the Sparks power died out a long time ago — at least everyone thought it had, until my mom married an Opus."

"But not all hypnotists are related to the Opus and Sparks families," Dr. Pedroia reasoned.

"Those are just the two most powerful bloodlines," Jax agreed. "There are other big names — Yamamoto, El Alamein. Axel used to talk about the Arcanov family, which included the spy Mata Hari and Dr. Ivan Pavlov. No one knows much about the other Arcanovs, though. They were really mysterious."

"The army is putting together a hypnotic database for HoWaRD. Only Colonel Brassmeyer has seen it so far, but I'd like you to take a look when it's further along. You have a unique perspective — you've worked with Sentia, you had a close relationship with Axel Braintree, and, of course, your father has direct memories of his Opus family."

Jax fidgeted in his chair. "Yeah, maybe."

"You shouldn't take it so hard that Stanley was able to bend you. There's no hard-and-fast rule about who can mesmerize who. It doesn't make you weaker than him. You know how special you are."

"That's not it," Jax replied. "I don't care about Stanley. It's just that . . . well, I was hoping to get my parents out of here as soon as Colonel Brassmeyer gives the okay. And what you just said kind of sounds like I'm staying awhile."

Pedroia looked sympathetic. "I have something to tell you, and you're not going to like it. Two days ago, Elias Mako escaped from federal prison in Florida. No one has seen him since."

Jax turned pale. "I warned them! There's not a prison in the world that can hold Mako! You look him in the eye, and you're lost."

"So it isn't possible for you and your family to leave Fort Calhoun. You're stuck here, for your own safety."

Jax was bitter. "If Mako can get out of a maximum-security prison, what makes you think he can't get into a maximum-security army post?"

"Steps are being taken," the psychiatrist assured him.

Jax folded his arms. "What steps can stop a guy who can get inside your mind?"

"Manpower," Pedroia replied readily. "A sentry can be hypnotized. But if there are six or seven, he can't reach them all at the same time, especially if they've been briefed on who and what to look out for. Remember — no one can hypnotize a bullet."

Jax said nothing. More than once he had underestimated the power and resourcefulness of Elias Mako.

He couldn't make that mistake again.

8

The chopper cruised over the desert, endless miles of scrub cactus and infinite beige. Jax sat stifling in his seat, sipping on a bottle of water, waiting for Colonel Brassmeyer, the only other passenger, to tell him what this was all about.

The colonel sat stiffly, too — but then again, he always did. Stiff was his style. Jax had never seen him sleep, but he was willing to bet that the man even slept stiffly. When he died, they wouldn't have to wait for rigor mortis to set in. It was already there.

"Is this Arizona?" Jax guessed, raising his voice to be heard over the noise of the rotors.

The grunt from Brassmeyer could have been a yes or a no. Or possibly, "Call an ambulance; I'm being devoured by fire ants."

"Where are we going?"

"We're there," came the reply.

"Here? We're in the middle of nowhere!" And then Jax saw it. A town had appeared on the horizon. He blinked. No, it wasn't a town. It was more like someone had taken a small chunk of an existing city and plopped it down in the heart of the desert.

As the chopper approached, Jax could make out low apartment buildings, neighborhoods of small neat homes, and even stores and businesses. And there were people bustling through the streets, going about their business, walking with baby carriages and pets. There was even traffic on the roadways, although the entire place was maybe half a mile square.

"What *is* this?" Jax asked in bewilderment.

"I brought you here because I want you to know exactly what you're doing. This is Delta Prime, population seven hundred and fifty-three volunteers. This is an entirely artificial test community constructed to simulate a larger city."

"Yeah, but what does it have to do with me?" Jax asked.

Brassmeyer called up to the pilot. "Turn us around. We're done here."

"What do you mean, we're done?" Jax squeaked. "All I saw was a bunch of houses and buildings! You need me to do something, but I don't even understand what it is!"

The colonel offered up a thin-lipped smile. "Opus, welcome to Operation Aurora."

It was a setup that Jax had experienced once before — in New York City, at Dr. Mako's Sentia Institute. He was peering into the lens of a large video camera, and his face — liquid irises floating somewhere between green and blue — filled a monitor on the wall.

"Look into my eyes . . . closer. . . . You are very calm, very relaxed. . . ."

The military personnel in the room — Brassmeyer, Pedroia, and two others — were looking everywhere in the studio except at the monitor or directly at Jax. Even the soldier serving as cameraman didn't dare gaze into the viewfinder once the recording had started. This was Jackson Opus in full hypnotic mode, and no one wanted to be bent by mistake. The army had even invented a term for it: *collateral mesmerism*.

"Now, when I snap my fingers," Jax went on, "you will remember nothing of me or this message. Life will go on, as it always has, and you will be happy and contented — until Thursday, October Fourth, at exactly ten AM. At that time, you will stop whatever you're doing and remain absolutely still, until you hear these words: *Briar Rose*. Then, and only then, you will go back to your regular life as if nothing at all has occurred." He raised his hand to his chin and snapped his fingers.

Jax had never seen the colonel so enthusiastic.

"Outstanding! We'll broadcast this message on TV at Delta Prime regularly until zero hour. Then we can measure the results."

"What results?" Jax queried. "Whether or not everybody stopped? Why is that important?"

Colonel Brassmeyer was in a good mood. "We're assessing our capability to disrupt an entire population through hypnotism. It goes far beyond stopping. Drivers would cease driving, people on the streets would stand still, a man stepping into an elevator would be incapable of pressing a button, everything would grind to a halt. Even the people who are untouched by the post-hypnotic suggestion would be stuck in the gridlock. The population would be completely incapable of responding to an outside invasion. The military applications are astounding!"

Jax was torn. This was the first thing he'd ever done that Brassmeyer actually approved of. But the thought of being used as a weapon of war — of Jackson Opus having "military applications" — made his stomach queasy. Before, he'd been a puppet on a string; now he was a live grenade.

Captain Pedroia seemed to understand what he was feeling. "It will save lives, Jax. On both sides. Less resistance means less destruction, less shooting."

"So it'll conserve resources, too," Brassmeyer concluded, pleased.

Jax wasn't sold, but he had to admit that bending people to stand still and be invaded was better than commanding them to jump off buildings or harm themselves in some other way.

"When does the message start to run?" he asked.

"That's on a need-to-know basis," the colonel informed him.

"Well, I need to know," Jax insisted. "This kind of hypnotism comes with blowback. It's like I'm making a connection with every single person who's bent by the video. I could be getting images from seven hundred minds at the same time. It's pretty hard to take."

Brassmeyer leafed through his notes. "How come this isn't in any of our research?"

"It isn't exactly established science," Pedroia supplied. "Jax is the only one who's ever tried it."

"And I've only done it once before," Jax added.

"How did it affect you?" Brassmeyer inquired.

"It almost killed me," Jax said evenly.

The colonel directed his reply to Captain Pedroia. "See to it that it doesn't."

"Yes, sir," the psychiatrist acknowledged.

Jax shook his head in amazement. Only in the army could you be ordered not to die.

For Jax, the next several days were like living with a time bomb. He knew that his video message would be broadcast in Delta Prime at any moment, and that he would suffer horrible blowback. The fact that it hadn't happened yet only made it worse.

Waiting for the thing to happen was as bad as the thing itself. He knew that the mesmeric impressions would keep him awake, so he couldn't sleep just worrying about it. He also knew that the dizzying effect would take his appetite away, so he stopped eating in advance.

"Jax, what's wrong with you?" his mother demanded. "Are you sick?"

How could he ever explain it to her? No other mind-benders had experienced the kind of blowback that came from a mass remote hypnotism. He'd be going through it under a psychiatrist's care, surrounded by his family and an army post full of people. Yet he'd be enduring it alone.

Adding to his distress was the big shift in power at HoWaRD. Suddenly, everything orbited little Stanley X. And it was Stanley, not Jax, who disappeared for long sessions with Colonel Brassmeyer.

"You're a has-been, Dopus," Wilson said cheerfully. "Or maybe more like a never-was."

Wilson had appointed himself Stanley's best friend, which made Stanley insanely happy. While Stanley was off with Brassmeyer, Wilson peppered the group with glowing reports of the young boy's accomplishments, 90 percent of which had to be baloney.

"Stanley bent a quartermaster and got us free stuff."

"Stanley made a general gobble like a turkey."

"Stanley got the cook to fly in lobster for us."

"Stanley bent a sapper and made him disarm a warhead."

On Thursday, Brassmeyer revealed the army's hypnotic database, and the HoWaRDs spent the day in a classroom setting, sifting through this new information. The name Opus was all over it. Jax thought he'd studied most of mesmeric history, between Sentia and his private lessons with Axel Braintree. To his surprise, the army had managed to come up with a lot that was unknown to him.

There was a black-and-white picture of Gerald Opus, peering into the eyes of two explorers as they entered the bathyscaphe on the very first voyage to Challenger Deep, the deepest part of Earth's oceans. The caption suggested that they never would have been crazy enough to go if they hadn't been hypnotized.

There was an audio clip, circa 1932, of the unmistakable voice of Winston Churchill saying, "Your eyelids are growing heavy. . . ." It supposedly came from a moment when he was having an audience with King George V.

The oldest artifact was a series of cave paintings that seemed to depict one primitive man peering into the eyes of another. Right after that, the second man went out and did battle with a saber-toothed tiger. The last picture was of the tiger enjoying a meal.

Most startling of all was a grainy, sepia-tone photograph of the wedding of Irina Arcanov. Computer enhancement techniques had blown up the faces of the bride, groom, and wedding party. Kneeling at the front was the ring bearer, a boy of about eight or nine, with knee breeches, a lace collar, a page-boy haircut, and an owl-like expression.

He was a dead ringer for Stanley X.

"Whoa!" Wilson exclaimed, eyes wide.

The HoWaRDs all stared at the image on the big screen at the front of the room.

"Does this mean what I think it means?" mused Evelyn Lolis.

Captain Pedroia took note of their reaction. "So you see it, too. Obviously, we'll never know for sure because there's no DNA to test. But it seems like we've found a real live Arcanov." He smiled. "X marks the spot."

Stanley looked confused. "Is that good?"

"Of course it's good!" Wilson jumped in. "Being an Arcanov is a thousand times better than being a Dopus! Everybody knows that."

"Actually, we don't know much about the Arcanovs at all," Ray Finklemeyer put in. "Even at Sentia, we . . ." His voice trailed off. The army may have trusted him, but an association with the fugitive Elias Mako wasn't something to be proud of.

"You're right, Ray," the captain chimed in quickly. "The Arcanovs are still largely a mystery. But now everything we learn will give us insight into Stanley, and why his ability is so special. That's why the army continues to pump money into this research. Anything the Arcanovs could do, there's a chance Stanley can, too."

Stanley made a sour face at the image on the slide. "I don't like the haircut. It's a girl's haircut."

Everybody laughed.

"You don't have to have the haircut, dear," Eunice promised him in her grandmotherly tone.

That was the thing about an eight-year-old mind-bender. A connection to greatness wasn't as important as not looking like a dork.

9

The blowback still hadn't started when Jax was torn out of bed the next morning at four AM.

"Let's go, Opus. The colonel's waiting. And you know how patient he's not."

Jax blinked bleary eyes, trying to gain focus on the soldier who stood over his bed. "Doesn't the colonel sleep?"

"That's classified, kid. Hurry up."

Jax threw on some clothes. "Can I leave a note for my parents?"

"Sorry. No can do."

"But if they wake up and I'm not here, they'll worry."

"You'll have to take that up with the colonel. Let's go."

As the Jeep bore him across the darkened post, Jax's mind raced. Why did Brassmeyer need to see him *now*? What was so urgent that it couldn't wait at least until sunup? Maybe they were about to start airing the message, and the colonel wanted to observe the effect it had on Jax. But that didn't make sense. Why would they broadcast in the wee hours of the morning, when there was nobody awake in front of the TV to see it?

Instead of Brassmeyer's office at HoWaRD, the Jeep dropped Jax off at the helipad, where the colonel was pacing impatiently. Jax, whose socks didn't match, and who hadn't been allowed to drag a comb through his rats' nest of hair, couldn't help noticing that HoWaRD's commanding officer was perfectly shaved, coiffed, and turned out. He could have made the cover of a manual on spit and polish.

"Let's move," he ordered, waving Jax into the bubble chopper.

Jax stuck out his jaw. "Not till my parents know where I am."

"Captain Pedroia is ringing your doorbell as we speak."

"Okay, then," Jax conceded. "Where are we going?"

"I'll brief you on the way."

They were airborne, passing over the Oklahoma countryside, when Brassmeyer spoke again. "This is Operation Flower Power."

Jax frowned. "What happened to Operation Aurora?"

"That's still on. This is different. We're going to see if you can use your skills to get inside a high-security facility. That's why we had to drag you out of bed at four in the morning. We don't want any planning time. You've got to do it using your hypnotic skills and your wits."

"What secure facility?" Jax asked uneasily.

"It's not Gymboree, believe me," the colonel replied. "We're going to the secure data storage center for military intelligence. They *will* shoot you. Make no mistake about that. So don't mess it up."

Jax felt a chill climbing up his spine. "What do I have to do?"

"You have to get past security" — Brassmeyer handed him a plastic Walmart shopping bag containing an old-fashioned alarm clock with a circular analog face and a double-bell ringer — "with this."

Jax was mystified. "Why?"

"Can't you tell? Security will take one look at this thing and assume it's a bomb. If you can hypnotize them to pass you through with *that*, then you can get in anywhere with anything."

"What if I can't bend them before they arrest me?" Jax queried nervously.

"That's what this exercise is designed to find out. Now — after you clear security, you make your way to the commander's office, and shoot him."

"Shoot him?" Jax echoed, horrified. "I can't kill anybody! I don't even step on ants!"

"Shoot him with this," Brassmeyer amended, grinning broadly. He held out a garish plastic daisy connected to a long clear plastic hose and a squeeze ball filled with water. He stuck the flower through Jax's buttonhole, running the tube underneath his shirt, and down into his pants pocket.

"A . . . squirt flower?"

"It's just another part of the exercise," Brassmeyer explained. "If you can get close enough to the commanding officer to give him a faceful of water, it'll be a perfect demonstration of what our Hypnotic Warfare unit is capable of."

"Squirting people," Jax repeated skeptically.

"Penetrating top security," the colonel amended. "Hypnotism was tailor-made for this. You're in and out without a shot being fired, and no one has any memory that you were ever there."

The Ryviker Military Data Storage Center was located outside Little Rock, Arkansas. It was a six-story structure that could have been a small office building, except that it was completely unmarked, and surrounded by a wide perimeter.

The chopper landed at a municipal helipad, and Brassmeyer drove out to the facility in a rental car. A quarter mile short of the gate, the colonel pulled onto the shoulder. "This is your stop."

"Aren't you coming?" Jax asked in alarm.

"You're the one breaking in, not me. I've got security clearance."

"But — they'll know something's up! I'm a kid walking down the road with an alarm clock in a Walmart bag like some random hobo! It'll be obvious something's weird."

"Exactly," Brassmeyer agreed. "Use your skills to get past that. You have to make them think that letting you in is the most natural thing in the world. I'll pick you up back here. Good luck."

Before Jax knew it, the colonel made a tight U-turn and drove away, and he was walking down a lonely road in the middle of Arkansas toward a gate manned by soldiers with guns. The morning sun had just cleared the horizon.

Jax had been through a lot of peculiar experiences since discovering he was a mind-bender, but this one was right up there.

There were three sentries in the gatehouse, one of them equipped with a large assault rifle. In addition, they were able to watch his approach along the deserted road, step by agonizing step, for at least ten minutes before he got anywhere near them. The gun wasn't actually pointed at him, but he couldn't shake the image of the crosshairs trained on his forehead.

The problem was clear: There were three guards, and he could only bend them one at a time. It was ironic. At Delta Prime, Jax's video was going to hypnotize seven hundred and fifty-three people almost simultaneously. Yet here he was, stymied by three.

That was when he saw it. About forty feet before the gate, a camera was stationed to give the sentries an advance peek inside any approaching vehicles. Jax bent down and peered directly into the lens, gambling that the sentries would check the monitor to see what he was doing.

A PIP image appeared almost immediately. It was grainy, Jax's face in close-up, framed by the monitor in the guard station. He had one of them. He bore down, leaning further into the camera. A second PIP appeared, from a slightly different angle. Two of the three were bent, but that wasn't good enough. He maneuvered himself so close to the lens that his color-changing eyes filled the monitor entirely. He could see that in the two images he'd already captured.

Come on, he implored the third man. *Look at the screen — just for a second! That's all I need!*

The guy wasn't coming. How long before he discovered there was something wrong with his two partners? Of course, Jax could sprint to the gate and bend the third man in person. But how would he know which of the three was still unbent?

A third PIP image, very faint, appeared between the other two. It winked out, reappeared, and stabilized. The bag with the clock tucked under his arm like a football, Jax sprinted the forty feet to the gatehouse. Now he was face-to-face with all three of them, huffing and puffing, but in control.

"Look into my eyes," he panted. It was a little disorienting to shift their attention from the monitor to his actual face, but he was able to swing the transition without losing any of them.

"You don't see me. I don't exist. You never admitted me through this gate," he told them. "But you" — he read the closest ID tag — "Staff Sergeant Ortiz, you have urgent business at the main building. You have to get there as soon as possible. Take the Jeep."

The instruction nearly worked too well. Sergeant Ortiz ran for the Jeep so quickly that Jax barely had a chance to get himself on board. Clutching the bag, he was still squirming over the spare tire into the backseat as the vehicle roared off up the road. The other two sentries watched benignly. They did not see the intruder hanging off the back of the Jeep. The hypnotic command was in full force. In their eyes, he did not exist.

As Ortiz approached the main entrance of the Ryviker facility, Jax labored to get his breathing under control. Hypnotic power was only one component of his bag of tricks. He also needed to be able to communicate clear instructions to his subjects. That wouldn't be possible if he couldn't catch his own breath. And he had a sinking feeling that the next little while would test his powers as they'd never been tested before.

When the Jeep came to a halt, Jax jumped out, alert for his next challenge. Sergeant Ortiz fidgeted at the wheel, frowning deeply. He'd been bent to believe he had urgent business, but hadn't been told what it was. This often happened when a hypnotic command was not specific enough. It was a loose end that Jax could not leave hanging.

"You're done here. You can go back to the gate." Jax had to scramble to get out of the way of the Jeep, which very nearly ran him down. The original command was still holding. Ortiz couldn't see him.

Through the sliding glass doors, Jax spied his next obstacle: a security desk with an officer checking IDs. He had none, and no business being there either, other than his mission.

At least it was only one person on duty this time, instead of three. She was a master corporal MP, and her brow furrowed at the sight of a twelve-year-old entering this very adult, very military facility.

"All right, kid. What's in the bag?"

Jax gave her his sweetest smile and made sure his eye

contact was a little more than just friendly. "My lunch," he told her. "Peanut-butter sandwich and a Twinkie."

When the MP opened the Walmart bag to reveal the clock, a peanut-butter sandwich and a Twinkie were exactly what she saw.

"You're very relaxed, very laid-back," Jax informed her. "You've already seen my ID, and it explains everything about what I'm doing here. Now please point me in the direction of the commander's office."

She pointed toward the elevator. "Fourth floor. Major Widmark is in suite four-twenty."

Jax's heart sank. Between here and the way up was a fully staffed security checkpoint, complete with metal detector and X-ray machine.

He placed the Walmart bag on the conveyor belt, knowing that the alarm clock wasn't going to be a big hit with the crew. As it disappeared inside the body of the scanner, Jax surveyed the checkpoint. There were four personnel. He could easily bend any one of them, but he needed to find the *right* one — the guard who was watching the monitor. In a matter of seconds, something was about to appear on that screen that greatly resembled a bomb. After that, things were going to get complicated real fast.

The monitor was located on the other side of the machine. Which meant that the soldier about to get an eyeful of alarm clock was on the other side, too — out of Jax's field of vision. It was a real dilemma. Jax couldn't very well bend the guy if he couldn't make eye contact.

Under the conveyor belt, Jax spotted the bottom of the man's chair and a pair of shiny black boots. The boots jumped as the soldier leaped to his feet. "Hey —!"

Think fast, Jax told himself. *Do something while you still can!*

That was when he noticed the mirror. It was on the wall outside the elevator, providing a view around the corner. Jax couldn't see himself in it, but he could see the man, whose mouth was already open to sound the alarm.

And if I can see him, then he can see me.

10

Jax locked his eyes on the man's image in the mirror, praying that the wide-angle glass would reflect his mesmeric thunderbolt to its target. There was no time to wait for a PIP. "That's my lunch in the Walmart bag!" he complained loudly, struggling to conceal his hypnotic instruction in what sounded like real conversation. "Is it okay to eat after X-rays go into it?"

There were chuckles around the checkpoint, but not a word from the man behind the machine. The Walmart bag waited at the far end of the conveyor belt.

Jax passed through the metal detector without incident, but another agent noticed the bulge in his pocket where the water bulb of his squirt flower was hidden.

"What's that?"

Nimbly, Jax broke the mesmeric connection with the scanner man and bent this new questioner. "I have no idea what you're talking about. There's nothing in my pocket."

"There's nothing in your pocket," the man agreed, waving him on.

He retrieved the bag and stepped into the elevator.

When the doors closed in front of him, he practically collapsed with relief. He held it together, though, when he noticed a security camera mounted in the corner. Was there no way to escape from prying eyes in this place?

He peered directly into the small lens with as much intensity as he could still muster after all the bending he'd done to get himself this far. Seriously, this had to be some kind of record! He breathed a silent apology to Axel Braintree, who had devoted his life to keeping his Sandmen honest.

The picture-in-picture image took longer than Jax expected, and he soon saw why. His face was on a monitor in a bank of several screens providing views throughout the building. He was surprised he had gotten attention as quickly as he had. He leaned into the camera, and very slowly and carefully mouthed the words: *There is no one on this elevator.*

He got off at the fourth floor, which was not nearly as deserted as he would have wished it to be. A kid with a Walmart bag drew a lot of stares, but no one stopped to question him. The Ryviker facility had so much security that anyone who'd made it to this point was assumed to have the right to be here, kid or not.

Jax followed the numbers on the doors until he reached suite 420. A brass plate on the wall announced: C.O. MAJOR JONATHAN WIDMARK. There was an outer office where a young man in uniform worked at a computer.

Jax entered, eyes blazing. The aide was bent almost immediately. "You never saw me," Jax told him. "I was never in this office." He set the Walmart bag down on the desk. "And don't touch my clock."

He headed for the door to the inner office, fingering the rubber bulb in his pocket. He felt an unexpected rush of exhilaration. He'd done it! As much as he hated Brassmeyer's idea of using hypnotism as a military weapon, how could he ignore the results? He had made it through multiple layers of security using nothing but the power of his mind. The old Jackson Opus, New York City middle schooler, never could have imagined it would be possible, much less that he would be the one who could pull it off.

He burst into the C.O.'s inner office and marched up to the desk where the major sat studying an open file in front of him. "Yes, Parker?" He looked up and saw not his assistant, but Jax. "What —?"

Jax squeezed the bulb. A jet of water shot from the plastic daisy on his chest and caught the major full in the face. For a split second, the C.O. was too shocked to respond. Then he lunged across the desk at Jax, uttering a string of curses. Jax danced back a step and locked his gaze on the major. But the subject was blinking water out of his eyes, and Jax could not get through to him.

He tried again, and this time a PIP image began to appear. "You are very relaxed," he intoned.

"I'm pretty far from relaxed!" sputtered the major. "Relaxed is the last thing I am! Who are you? How did you get in here?"

"You don't see me," Jax persisted.

"What in blue blazes are you raving about? *Security!*"

Jax was bewildered. Why wasn't the major following his instructions? He had to be bent. Where else could this PIP be coming from?

That was when he noticed that the PIP image was . . . wrong. It wasn't Major Widmark's view of Jax in the office; it was a different room altogether. There was a TV, and on that TV —

Oh, no! he thought, numb with horror. *Not today! Not now!*

On that TV was Jax himself, in the video he'd recorded for Operation Aurora. They were playing it in Delta Prime. The blowback was beginning! Even as that thought crossed his mind, the image doubled, and then doubled again — different rooms, but the same Jax on TV.

You can't worry about that! Jax exhorted himself. *Bend Widmark! Concentrate on here and now!*

But by the time he tried to refocus on the major, at least a dozen PIPs filled his field of vision, leaving him dizzy and half blind.

He heard rather than saw the MPs storm the room. Rough hands grabbed him, threw him to the floor, and flipped him over on his face. He felt his arms pinned behind him as cuffs were slapped on his wrists. Hypnotism was out of the question now. All he could see was the carpet.

"All right," said the major in a no-nonsense voice. "The jig is up."

11

Throughout the interrogation, Jax remained handcuffed to a high-back wooden chair.

"Who are you, and what are you doing here?"

Jax didn't answer, and not just because he was being bombarded by mesmeric impressions from Delta Prime. The Hypnotic Warfare Research Department was top secret. Brassmeyer was constantly drilling into the HoWaRDs' heads that they were absolutely forbidden to discuss it with anyone, even the non-HoWaRD army personnel at Fort Calhoun.

"Who sent you?"

Again, silence. It would have been so much easier just to bend Widmark, but he couldn't — not with two armed MPs standing there watching.

"What's in that clock?"

Finally, something Jax could answer. "It's just a clock."

"What did you spray me with?"

"Water."

"Do you expect me to believe that?"

A shrug.

"What did you do to my aide?"

"I didn't hurt him," Jax defended himself.

"He claims he never even saw you, and you must have passed within three feet of his chair! And when I asked him to move the alarm clock, he defied a direct order. Then he burst into tears like a two-year-old. Parker's a good man! I want an explanation!"

Jax felt bad about that. He had specifically commanded Parker not to touch the clock. To be placed in conflict between a hypnotic order and a military one could tear a soldier in two. No wonder the poor guy cried.

"He didn't do anything wrong," Jax said. "It wasn't his fault."

"Now we're getting somewhere," the major barked. "Whose fault was it?"

Back to silence.

"I called down to the desk to ask who admitted a young boy. And you know what they told me? There was no young boy! How did you get in here? The same way you managed to ghost-walk past Parker?"

There was a knock at the door, and a technician in a voluminous silver hazmat suit waddled in. He flipped up the face guard. "All clear, sir. The clock is clean — old-school analog alarm clock with a mechanical bell."

"What about radiation?" Widmark persisted.

"The Geiger counter says it's clear," Hazmat reported. "And the squirt flower was standard joke-shop stuff, filled with pure H_2O. Nothing to worry about."

The major clearly thought he should be worrying about something. The fact that there was nothing was even more disturbing.

"This isn't over," he told Jax when the technician was gone. "I'm going to get to the bottom of this — don't think I won't."

Through the storm of blowback from fourteen hundred miles away, Jax wondered how scared he should be. He hadn't mentioned Brassmeyer or HoWaRD so far. But surely there would soon be a time when his responsibility to protect the secret installation at Fort Calhoun would come second to his responsibility to protect himself. He had broken into a secure facility. You could go to jail for that, especially since Widmark was absolutely convinced that something sinister was at play here. Jax had the perfect explanation all cued up: He had done it on a direct order from a US Army colonel. Except *that* order violated another order to keep HoWaRD secret. And there were probably consequences for breaking that one, too.

Eventually, they brought him to a small basement holding cell, took away his belt and shoelaces, and locked him inside. He was there for hours, hungry, thirsty, and scared to death. On top of it all, the blowback came in waves every time his hypnotic message was rebroadcast in Delta Prime. As the day drew on and TV viewership grew, there were so many images that they melted into a Technicolor collage that blurred his vision and gave him unbearable headaches.

The clatter of heavy boots on the concrete floor snapped Jax out of his misery. Two extra-large MPs wearing mirrored sunglasses opened the door of the cell. Jax noted that these were new men, not the pair that had manhandled him in Widmark's office and brought him here.

"Time to go, kid."

"Where am I going?" Jax asked in a small voice.

There was no answer. Jax couldn't help feeling a stab of sympathy for Major Widmark, who was also not getting any answers, through no fault of his own.

The MPs put the handcuffs back on, and then things got really scary. One of them slipped a black hood over Jax's head.

"What's that for?" Jax quavered, terrified.

"Sorry, kid. We've got our orders."

"From who? Darth Vader?"

"Nothing personal, but if you're going to make a fuss, we'll have to gag you."

The experience of being marched blindly out of the building was more terrifying than anything Jax could remember. He could feel the fresh air when they stepped outside. It didn't last long. He was thrown in the back of some kind of vehicle, and sensed darkness when the door was slammed behind him. Then they were driving, with one brief stop — the gatehouse? The agony of being left guessing at what fate awaited him was worse than any torture the army could have dreamed up.

Where are they taking me? he thought desperately. *Some secret prison? Or worse? Will I ever see my family again?*

He made up his mind then and there that all promises to Brassmeyer were off the table. He had to do everything he could to save himself.

It seemed like hours later, but was probably only fifteen minutes, when they stopped again. Jax heard the door being opened, felt air touch his exposed skin.

"Is anybody there?" And when strong hands grabbed him and dragged him out of the vehicle, Jax knew it was now or never. He might not get another chance to explain himself.

"None of this is my fault! Call Colonel Roderick Brassmeyer! He runs the Hypnotic Warfare Research Department at Fort Calhoun! If you haven't heard of it, it's because it's top secret —"

The hood was yanked from his head, and he found himself practically nose-to-nose with Brassmeyer himself.

The colonel's face was a thundercloud. "What part of 'classified information' don't you understand, Opus?"

Conflicting emotions bubbled up in Jax — relief at being out of Ryviker, embarrassment at spilling the beans in front of the very person who'd ordered him not to, mental exhaustion from the ordeal he'd just been through and the blowback that continued to haunt him.

He opened his mouth to apologize, and what came out was a tirade that even he hadn't known was lurking there.

"They arrested me! They handcuffed me! They put me in a cell! And then there was a hood on my head, and no one would tell me anything, and I didn't know if I'd ever see my mom and dad again!" There was more, but he never managed to get it out, because the stress of the day caught up with him, and he broke down.

Brassmeyer produced a key and freed him from the handcuffs. "You didn't know I'd be coming for you? How could you think I'd launch an operation without a contingency for that? You're a valuable asset!"

"But I was in there for hours!"

"That's how long it took me to pull the strings to shake you loose! Do you think I've got the juice to waltz out of there with a prisoner just because I've got birds on my collar? You don't know the army very well. You've got to be God to make things happen — or at least a general."

"It's your fault I got caught," Jax quavered. "I made it all the way to the C.O., shot him with the squirt flower, and I was just about to bend him when I got blowback from Delta Prime! I told you about blowback, how bad it is! If I'm so valuable, why don't you listen to me?"

"Operation Aurora started broadcasting your message this morning," the colonel said solemnly.

"Well, I know that!" Jax shot back. "It practically blew my head off! And by the time I recovered, two MPs were sitting on me, pushing my face into the carpet!"

Brassmeyer was silent for a long moment. Then he said the last thing Jax expected.

"Sorry."

Jax was amazed. Brassmeyer never apologized, not even when he'd backed a Jeep over Pedroia's Vespa.

"I've been in the army too long," the colonel went on. "A soldier is used to being told only his own tiny part of things. Sometimes he's expected to risk his life without ever knowing the big picture of what it's all about. But you're not a soldier. And you're also a kid. I shouldn't have hung you out to dry without making sure you understood absolutely that I had your six."

"My six?"

"You know — your six o'clock, your hind end. Now tell me about this blowback."

"It comes in waves every time the video airs in Delta Prime," Jax explained. "The more people who are bent by it, the more images I get. It's usually just a jumble, kind of a blur of color and motion. But after a while, it gets physical, like you have the flu — headaches, shakes, dizziness, nausea. I had this once in New York. I fell down the stairs in my school and ended up in the hospital."

Brassmeyer thought it over. "We can't pull the plug on Aurora," he said finally. "The exercise is just too important. We built a whole town for it."

"I don't think I'm going to be much use to you until after October Fourth," Jax warned, massaging his temples.

"Take some Tylenol," Brassmeyer advised. "And stay away from stairs."

12

"I'm not sick, Mom," Jax told his mother through the steam of a bowl of chicken soup. "You know exactly what's wrong with me."

Undaunted, Monica Opus ladled out two more bowls, one for herself and another for her husband. "You're not feeling well. What difference does it make if it comes from a germ or from some of that hocus-pocus?"

Resignedly, Jax took a taste, and burned his tongue.

The blowback from Delta Prime had been getting worse as October Fourth approached, and Jax's hypnotic message was broadcast with ever-greater frequency. It didn't matter that there were only seven hundred and fifty-three people in the test community. Every time they were exposed to the video clip, they were bent anew, and that mesmeric link rebounded to Jax. Late-night airings made sleep impossible. Just as he'd be about to drop off to uneasy dreams, some night owl's mind would reach out to him through the link. And what little rest he could get would be cut short, because there were always the early risers watching TV with their morning joe.

"Ashton!" called Mrs. Opus. "Soup's on."

"Be right there," came the reply from another room. There was a crash, followed by the tinkle of broken glass.

Jax and his mother exchanged a long-suffering look. In the ongoing struggle to fight the boredom of Fort Calhoun, Dad's latest obsession was a FreeForAll game called Virtual Tiffany, in which players designed elaborate stained-glass windows, lamps, and chandeliers.

Ashton Opus slouched into the kitchen. "That site is such a rip-off," he complained. "Everything is supposed to be free, but it costs eight bucks to upgrade your dustpan if you get glass on the floor."

"Have some soup," his wife suggested.

Mr. Opus regarded Jax. "Feeling any better?"

"A little," Jax lied.

"My parents never got sick from any blowback," his father muttered. He looked thoughtful. "Then again, maybe they did, and I don't remember it because they helped me forget it. I didn't remember the ballet lessons either until I saw that picture of myself onstage in tights."

"Your parents didn't get blowback, Dad," Jax reminded him. "It comes from remote hypnotism. I'm the only one who's done that so far."

"Well, stop doing it!" his mother said sharply.

"Tell that to the army," said Jax bitterly. "They send people into war zones. So if all I get from them is a headache, I'm ahead of the game."

"Colonel Brassmeyer should be ashamed of himself for

putting you through all this," his mother persisted. "I'd like to give him a piece of my mind."

"Yeah, good luck with that," her son told her, rubbing his forehead. "Anyway, he hasn't been around too much lately. He's got a big exercise coming up."

The colonel's absences had little to do with Operation Aurora. Brassmeyer had been taking a number of small trips with Stanley X. More than once, Jax spotted the two of them at the helipad, waiting for their lift to who knew where.

Jax found himself resenting the eight-year-old, which was unfair. It wasn't Stanley's fault he'd bent Jax that time. Jax never questioned the fact that he so easily dominated most of the others. But *being* dominated — and by a little kid — rankled him.

A valuable asset, Brassmeyer had called him. But was Stanley more valuable now?

What do you care? Jax demanded of himself. *Let Stanley have the spotlight. You hate the army!*

But it was impossible not to enjoy the admiration. Jax had basked in the praise of the HoWaRD officers while making his report on Operation Flower Power. There had been laughter and applause as he'd described squirting Major Widmark. Everyone agreed that the exercise would have been a total success if it hadn't been for the untimely burst of blowback. Jax would have hypnotized the C.O., and then retraced his steps along the trail of security guards he'd bent on the way in.

Jax didn't mention that if he could bend his way into the Ryviker facility, the newly free Elias Mako could do the same to gain access to Fort Calhoun. Mako was the most cunning mind-bender who had ever lived.

With Brassmeyer and Stanley out of town, HoWaRD continued to focus on the army's hypnotic database. Jax was interested to learn more about the Arcanovs, but the blowback made it difficult for him to read anything off a screen.

It must have been obvious how much Jax was suffering because even Wilson noticed.

"What's the matter, Dopus? You look terrible."

"Since when do you care if I'm sick?"

"I don't think you're sick. There's stuff you do that nobody else can, and I remember the effect it had on you. What's Colonel Rod got you up to?"

"If Colonel Rod wanted you to know, he'd tell you," Jax shot back.

Wilson raised an eyebrow. "So you *are* working on something special. I remember you stumbling around Sentia, green in the face because Mako made you a video star. I think Rod's trying the same thing."

"You don't know what you're talking —" He never finished the sentence, because at that moment, a fresh wave of mesmeric images hit. Jax wasn't sure which bothered him more — the blowback itself, or the fact that it made him let his guard down. How could he be reckless enough not to watch what he was saying around Wilson, who was not only an enemy, but who had once had such strong ties to Mako?

"Oh, that looked real painful," Wilson said in mock sympathy. "It must have been a bad one."

Jax gagged once, lurched forward, and threw up all over Wilson's army boots.

13

By the morning of Thursday, October 4, Jax was so ill that Brassmeyer had to help him into the helicopter. By this time, even the colonel was concerned.

"Geez, kid, you've aged thirty years since all this started! I think you're losing weight, too! What can we do to help you?"

Jax just shrugged and took his seat. He had told the colonel again and again what was causing all this. If the man didn't understand it by now, he never would.

The flight to the desert southwest was just a blur. At first, Jax was too weak to speak. But as they crossed into Arizona, his headache lessened, the nausea receded, and his vision began to clear. By the time it occurred to Jax that he was starting to feel better, he was 100 percent fine.

He turned to Brassmeyer. "They took the messages off the air, right?"

"The last one aired at nine twenty-two," the colonel confirmed. "I wondered if you'd notice."

Jax bit his tongue. Yeah, he noticed — the way a drowning man notices when he's pulled out of the water. *Put that in your database, Roderick.*

Soon the artificial community appeared on the horizon. Brassmeyer tapped the pilot's shoulder. "Take us in closer, and circle."

As they approached Delta Prime, Jax could make out the individual buildings and roads. It was a busy place, bustling like the kind of city it had been created to simulate. The chopper descended a little more, and they could see pedestrians coming and going.

Jax checked his watch. 9:46. Fourteen minutes to go. Although he had barely given a thought to Operation Aurora beyond his own misery, he was suddenly filled with a burning curiosity about what would happen when ten o'clock rolled around.

"How do you think it's going to go?" he asked the colonel.

"That's why we do the exercise," came the reply. He produced two sets of binoculars and handed one to Jax.

Jax peered through the field glasses. They gave him a perfect street-level view. A woman walked a large Doberman, a workman started up a light pole, a couple pushed a baby carriage, a grocery-delivery boy rode by on a bike.

"Two minutes," murmured the colonel.

It all looked so *normal* that Jax couldn't imagine what might possibly happen here that had a senior military officer hovering in a helicopter, waiting with bated breath.

"Ten seconds," Brassmeyer intoned.

Jax counted down in his mind. Three seconds — two — one —

The people stopped.

All over the streets, they stood, not frozen exactly, but unmoving. The cars continued to roll as drivers let up on the gas and ceased steering. There were fender benders and collisions. One car jumped the curb, flattened a fire hydrant, and went into a shop through a plate-glass window. The hydrant sent jets of water in all directions. Pedestrians were being drenched, but no one moved to get away from the spray.

Jax picked up the binoculars for a closer look. The bike messenger stopped pedaling, coasted to a halt, and keeled over into a flowerbed. The Doberman was on its hind legs, frantically licking its owner's face in search of signs of life. The animal seemed to be howling. The parents stood passively by, oblivious to the presence of their baby or each other.

"Outstanding!" breathed Brassmeyer.

About a half-dozen people apparently hadn't been affected by the post-hypnotic suggestion. They were running around amid the "statues," yelling into faces and shaking arms and shoulders in search of some kind of reaction. They were joined by others, running out of houses and buildings in search of some kind of clue as to what was going on. Their panic was evident. Many screamed into cell phones, trying to sound the alarm.

Black smoke began to pour out of a small luncheonette. A group of the unaffected rushed inside and began dragging out immobile customers and employees. Those being rescued offered no help. Jax's hypnotic command prevented them from moving, even to save their own lives. Seconds later, the storefront was engulfed in flames. The firehouse was barely half a block away, but no one came.

"We've got to wake these people up!" Jax said urgently. "Come on — give the trigger word! Snap them out of it!"

The colonel tossed him a dismissive gesture, eyes never leaving his binoculars.

"If you won't do it, I will!" Jax undid his seat belt, stuck his head out the side of the bubble, and bellowed, *"Briar Rose! Briar Rose!"* His voice never made it past the clatter of the rotor blades.

Red with rage, Brassmeyer grabbed him by the belt and yanked him back into his seat like he was a rag doll. "Try that again, mister, and you'll be in restraints!"

"But I did this!" Jax wailed. "This is my fault!"

"It was *my* order," Brassmeyer amended. "You did what you were told. For once."

"But someone's going to get *killed*!"

"Let me worry about that!"

That was the trouble, Jax thought desperately. Brassmeyer *wasn't* going to worry about it. He was in a business where sacrificing lives was all part of a chess game.

I know a way to make him listen to me!

He turned blazing eyes on the colonel.

With the reaction time of a striking cobra, Brassmeyer's meaty hand snapped out and covered Jax's face. "Do you honestly believe I could spend time around mind-benders and never give a thought to what I would do if any of the nine of you decided to try something like that?" His hand was pressing hard, imprisoning Jax against the seat. "I'm going to pretend that little stunt never happened. But mark my words — if you ever get out of line again, you're gone. And you might want to think about how you and your family will get along without military protection now that Dr. Mako is on the loose. Am I going to have a problem when I take my hand away?"

"No," Jax barely whispered.

By now several plumes of smoke reached skyward from houses and buildings in Delta Prime. Reports were coming in from a mobile command center that was monitoring cameras strategically placed around the town. There were fires started by unattended cooking, and floods from sinks and bathtubs left running. Injuries were widespread, mostly minor falls. But the military personnel were keeping an eye on a few situations that were potentially more dangerous.

"Should we move in and try to extract the more serious cases?" came the voice from the command center.

"Not yet," was Brassmeyer's decision. "Let's not contaminate the experiment until it becomes absolutely necessary."

Jax was horrified. People were suffering down there, and for what? The experiment was over, wasn't it? The hypnotic "attack" had worked. To leave victims twisting in the wind when you had the power to help them was cruel and unnecessary. But he didn't dare try to argue with the colonel after their last exchange.

When the experiment reached the fifteen-minute mark, Colonel Brassmeyer ordered the pilot to land. The chopper set down about a mile away from Delta Prime, next to the cluster of tents that represented the mobile command center. There were at least a dozen other helicopters standing by.

One tent seemed to be some kind of field hospital. Another was the command center itself. Inside, soldiers followed video feeds coming in from all over the town. Watching them made Jax feel crushing remorse. One screen showed a howling toddler desperately trying to rouse his mother from her mysterious stupor. A pile of people sat at the bottom of an escalator where the moving staircase had deposited them. A forklift truck pushed up against a wall, its driver immobile at the controls. The wheels spun relentlessly, clouds of burning rubber rising from the tires. In a supermarket, an automatic meat slicer worked its way through an entire corned beef brisket and kept on slicing.

Jax cringed as monitors all around the tent showed electrical transformers sizzling, sparking, and exploding. On one of them, Jax noticed the pole worker tossed from his position at the box. He hung limply from his safety belt, unmoving.

The true purpose of Operation Aurora began to sink in at that moment. The post-hypnotic suggestion to stop dead was more than a tactic to disable a town's resistance; it was a weapon of mass destruction, and the proof of it was right before his eyes. Electrical explosions, fires, floods, accidents; a population unable to move, much less defend itself.

After half an hour, the colonel gave the order to send individual teams into Delta Prime to rescue anyone they deemed to be in serious danger. The helicopters came back bearing the dangling pole worker; the baby in the carriage, who was being doused with ice-cold water from the hydrant; and a man who had been halfway down a flight of stairs when ten o'clock hit, and had tumbled to the bottom. There were also cases of smoke inhalation and some minor burns. Next door at the field hospital, doctors greeted the wounded with the words "Briar Rose," neutralizing the post-hypnotic suggestions so that the patients could wake up and receive treatment.

Still, Brassmeyer refused to do anything to help the several dozen people who were unaffected, and who were becoming wildly hysterical as they watched their town fall apart, and their neighbors and loved ones fail to snap out of this immobile and unreachable state. Eleven o'clock came and went, and there was still no mercy for Delta Prime. The broken fire hydrant stopped spewing, signifying the end of the town's limited water supply. Fires spread from building to building, house to house. Choppers bore more and more evacuees to the field hospital.

"Are you just going to let it all *burn*?" Jax pleaded.

"It's not a real town, Opus," the colonel told him patiently. "Nobody lives here. These people are all volunteers."

"But they didn't know they were volunteering for *this*!"

At that moment, the trapped forklift broke through the prefab wall it had been pushing against. The machine disappeared in an avalanche of plaster and lumber. In what looked like slow motion, the entire building collapsed in on itself. In another monitor, clouds of dust and debris obscured the street. When it dissipated, the people were still there, still unmoving, covered in a layer of white. The terrified Doberman, also powdered white, cowered by its mistress.

Brassmeyer consulted his watch. "Mark the time — eleven twenty-three. I'm pulling the plug on Aurora. Give the signal."

The Arizona sky turned beige with sand and dirt as the entire fleet of choppers lifted off and headed to the devastated town. Minutes later, the loudspeakers echoed around the desert.

"Briar rose. Briar rose. Briar rose."

Jax watched the monitors as the living dead of Delta Prime came back to life amid the wreckage of their temporary home.

14

"Really, Wilson?"

Wilson slouched in his chair in Captain Pedroia's office, his black boots — carefully cleaned and spit-shined after Jax had thrown up on them — on the desk.

"Whatever," Wilson mumbled, unfolding his long legs and bringing them down to the floor. He hated his regular sessions with HoWaRD's psychiatrist, but there was no getting out of them.

"It must be hard being here without your family," Pedroia began.

Wilson shrugged. "At least I don't have parents running my life and sticking their noses where they don't belong."

"No," Pedroia agreed in amusement. "You have the US Army doing that now. And you might have noticed that they're pretty good at it."

Another shrug. "I like the army. They blow stuff up."

"And how do you find living on your own?" the psychiatrist persisted.

"I'm not homesick, if that's what you mean."

"But surely it's a huge adjustment."

"What, you think Stanley can hack it, but not me?"

"Stanley's not on his own; he's with me," Pedroia reminded him. "And besides, he's a special case. He's never had a family."

"Except the Arcanovs."

"You know what I mean. He's never lived with parents. He's bounced around orphanages his whole life."

"Boo-hoo," Wilson drawled.

The psychiatrist frowned. "I thought you liked Stanley."

"Stan's the *man*," Wilson said positively. "About time somebody took Dopus to school."

Pedroia leaned back in his chair. "Did it ever occur to you that your friendship with Stanley isn't a friendship at all? Maybe he just makes you feel better about the inferiority complex you have for Jax."

Wilson was silent a moment. Then, "Wow, doc, you must be a genius. Did they teach you all that in college?"

"I'm not an idiot, and neither are you. It's no disgrace that Jax's powers are greater than yours, but for some reason, you can't get past it. Who are you trying to impress, Wilson? Not me, obviously. Is it the colonel? The army?" The psychiatrist stood up. "Or are you proving yourself to someone who picked Jax over you a long time ago? Someone like . . . Dr. Mako?"

"Come to think of it, where is Dopus?" asked Wilson. "He's been gone since yesterday."

"That's none of your business. It's classified."

"I'm *making* it my business." Suddenly, Wilson leaped

out of his chair and stared into Pedroia's eyes. The captain lashed out with his arm to block the mesmerizing gaze, but Wilson grabbed his wrist and forced it away. The psychiatrist was strong, but the young mind-bender only needed a few seconds. . . .

Wilson saw his own triumphant smile in the PIP image of himself from Pedroia's point of view. He may not be a rock star like Stanley or Dopus, but Wilson DeVries had been trained at Sentia, learning at the feet of Dr. Mako himself.

He leaned in to his subject's face. "Now you're going to tell me everything you know about where Jackson Opus is, and why he went there."

Completely bent, the psychiatrist was powerless to resist. "It's called Operation Aurora. . . ."

"By our calculations, the post-hypnotic suggestion reached seventy-nine percent of the population. We were expecting more, but some people don't watch TV, I guess. If we'd disseminated the message over the Internet as well, we feel we could have cracked ninety percent."

Colonel Brassmeyer had assembled all the officers of the Hypnotic Warfare Research Department in his office for this debriefing on Operation Aurora.

"Were there any casualties?" inquired Major Elizabeth Bigelow, who had been sent to this meeting to report back to the army chief of staff.

"There might have been," Brassmeyer replied, "but we stepped in when we thought life was at stake. We had about sixty injured, half of those from a building collapse. But let me tell you, that town is dust. Think about it — we didn't command those people to destroy anything. They were only hypnotized to stop what they were doing and stay still. And in less than two hours, the power had failed, the water was out, and what hadn't fallen apart was on fire."

"What's your assessment of the resistance we could expect from a population subjected to this kind of hypnotic attack?" Major Bigelow probed.

"An invading force would encounter negligible opposition," the colonel boasted. "The unaffected are too stunned by what's happened to everybody else to fight back. The biggest threat we encountered was a nervous dog. It would be a cakewalk."

Lieutenant Kyushu spoke up. He was in charge of statistical analysis for HoWaRD. "I've run some simulations, applying the Aurora numbers to larger population centers. For example, if the hypnotic message had been run in a city the size of New York, we could expect injuries into the hundreds of thousands including at least five hundred fatalities. Property damage would be estimated somewhere between thirty-five and sixty billion dollars."

"Of course," Brassmeyer conceded, "in a big city, it's impossible to allow for any difficulty we might have in delivering the trigger word to end the hypnoattack. In that case, the collateral damage would increase exponentially."

Bigelow seemed puzzled, so Captain Pedroia stepped in. "If we can't terminate the suggestion, we risk widespread deaths from dehydration. The hypnotized would stop still for days, unable to look after their most basic needs."

The major made notes. "So your invaders would need to bring a humanitarian force to minimize casualties among the innocent."

"I suppose," the colonel said impatiently. "But don't you see? This is a weapon the likes of which the world has never known! Whole cities could fall without a shot ever being fired!"

The major nodded. "Do I get to meet this Jackson Opus? I think the general would like to hear about the wonder boy who can make all this happen."

"Jax is a sensitive kid," Pedroia began carefully. "He was on site at Delta Prime, and it really upset him to see people suffering because of something he did."

"He'll get over it," Brassmeyer scoffed.

"I'm not so sure," Pedroia countered. "But one way or the other, it's not a good idea to have him revisit it so soon after the event. I recommend letting him cool off a little bit longer."

The colonel glared at him. "She's here representing a four-star general. She can see whoever she pleases."

"The general can wait," Bigelow assured him. "I'm a parent myself, and I know how twelve-year-olds can be. We have to be careful with this kid. After all, he's the only one capable of this kind of large-scale hypnotism."

There was a sudden awkward silence. The HoWaRD officers exchanged uncertain glances.

The major picked up on it immediately. "What am I missing here?"

Brassmeyer cleared his throat carefully. "Um — exactly how high is your security clearance?"

15

After Operation Aurora, Jax was given three days off before returning to the Hypnotic Warfare Research Department. This was on Captain Pedroia's recommendation. If it had been up to the colonel, the mind-benders would all have been digging trenches alongside the troops every minute that they weren't refining their mental powers.

Ray Finklemeyer and Jerry Katsakis were off working on a special project to determine whether a mesmeric command could improve soldiers' marksmanship. The others were at computers, studying the hypnotic database — all except Eunice, who didn't "do" technology, and was wading through a mountain of printed pages.

"Welcome back, dear," she called to Jax. "We heard you performed wonderfully well."

Jax was amazed. "The colonel said that?"

"Don't be ridiculous," she replied. "The colonel never says anything nice about anybody. But I saw him smile three times yesterday. That doesn't happen for nothing."

The mind-benders interrupted their research to greet Jax.

Wilson scowled at him. "You been away?"

Jax couldn't help noticing that Wilson's computer screen was not on the hypnotic database. He was on the FreeForAll website, playing a game called Gale Warning, where participants worked to create storms at sea and sink ships.

Jax looked around. "Where's Stanley?"

"What's the matter, Dopus?" sneered Wilson. "Eight-year-old got you spooked?"

"The colonel took him somewhere right after his trip with you," Evelyn Lolis supplied.

"But I just saw Brassmeyer by the PX," Jax persisted. "If he's here, where's Stanley?"

"It's no big deal," Wilson insisted. "The squirt's probably got himself another cold for a change."

But later, in the break room, Evelyn sidled up to Jax. "About Stanley — there's something fishy going on. I don't think he's coming back."

Jax was startled. "Why do you say that?"

"Ask any of them — the officers or the soldiers. You can't get an answer. It's like they don't know, but they do." She leaned down from her great height, which was at least six feet, and added in a whisper, "They're hiding something."

By the end of the week, Stanley still hadn't returned to Fort Calhoun. Brassmeyer was there — his foghorn voice could be heard echoing down every hallway and stairwell in the Hypnotic Warfare Research Department building. But the eight-year-old was nowhere to be found.

Speculation ran high. It wasn't unusual for one of the HoWaRDs to disappear for a day or two on special assignment, accompanied by a staff member. This time, though, the only one missing was the eight-year-old. And the army — from Brassmeyer down to the lowliest private — refused to say anything about it. Stanley's whereabouts were strictly on a need-to-know basis. None of the HoWaRDs needed to know.

Eunice was concerned that "the poor little soul" had suffered a mental collapse brought on by the pressure of his powers, and was recovering in a hospital somewhere. Jerry and Ray suspected that Stanley was off with a new guardian assigned by the army. Brassmeyer was too high up to spend his time nurse-maiding an eight-year-old, they argued. Dirk and Evelyn were convinced that the major who came around sometimes had taken Stanley to Washington to meet the top generals.

Wilson liked this idea best. "How come nobody ever took you to Washington, Dopus? Oh, yeah — because you stink at hypnotism and everybody knows it."

Even Anatoly seemed to have an opinion, although nobody understood it, since he expressed it in Romanian.

Captain Pedroia was becoming weary of the constant questioning. "When it's time for you to be told, you'll be told. That's how it works."

"But *when?*" Jax persisted during one of their private sessions.

"Probably never," the psychiatrist replied. "Am I ever going to know why my request for size eleven boots was denied? No, I'm going to cut my toenails very short and limp around in my ten-and-a-halfs. Welcome to the army. Why do you need to know?"

"Don't you get it?" Jax demanded. "Anything that happens to Stanley — it could just as easily happen to me! If he disappears one day, I could be next!"

"Why would you even think such a thing?" asked Pedroia in shock. "This is America! We don't do things like that!"

"Don't give me that," Jax shot back. "You've got nine of us here, supposedly of our own free will. We can leave anytime we want to — until we want to."

"Why would you want to?" asked Pedroia. "The security we offer you from Mako —"

"See, that's how you do it!" Jax cut him off. "It's not even whether or not I'm allowed to go. You never let the discussion get to that point. And that's you — a good guy. Think how the colonel would react."

The psychiatrist was quiet a moment. "Would it help if I assure you that Stanley is fine? Better than fine."

"I'd need to know whether it's fine fine or size-ten-and-a-half-boots fine."

The captain gave him a long look. Jax was taken aback. The HoWaRD staff had been trained to avoid direct eye contact with mind-benders, knowing how easy it would be for any of the nine to hypnotize them. Yet here was Pedroia practically inviting Jax to put him under and take the information he wanted.

Jax glanced away before the picture-in-picture image could fully form.

The psychiatrist sighed. "You have to do everything the hard way, don't you? Maybe you belong in the military." He took a deep breath. "What I'm about to tell you doesn't go past the walls of this office. Understood?"

"I won't tell anybody," Jax promised.

"The army hasn't done anything to Stanley. Some of the research that went into the hypnotic database dug up a distant relative."

"An Arcanov?" Jax asked.

Pedroia shook his head. "Just a regular guy. I think his name is Ferguson. I didn't meet him. Anyway, this guy was thrilled to find he has an eight-year-old cousin and he filed for adoption."

Jax was astounded. "And Brassmeyer agreed?"

"The colonel's not a monster. Who wouldn't want to see an orphan find a family who's going to raise him and care for him?"

"But Stanley's an asset!" Jax protested. "The army doesn't give those up. I'm living proof of that."

"You may not love Fort Calhoun, but you've got a family, and they're living right here with you. That poor little kid has never had anybody. What do you know — the army has a heart. Maybe not for a guy with sore feet, but they made the right call for Stanley when it really mattered." He leaned back in his chair, an expression of perplexity on his face. "Tell me something. Did I just give you all that because I decided to, or because you got into my head and made me do it?"

"That was all you," Jax promised.

The psychiatrist frowned. "How can I be sure of that?"

"Because if I'd bent you, I'd have made sure you forgot the whole conversation."

Since the Hypnotic Warfare Research Department was classified, few of the soldiers at Fort Calhoun had any idea what was going on in the wide, low building near the northwest corner of the post. So when Jax stepped into the quartermaster's stores that afternoon, the top sergeant at the desk saw only a very young civilian with a baseball cap pulled low over his face

"What can I do for you, kid?" The man yawned without much enthusiasm.

Jax surveyed the warehouse. The two of them were alone.

He flipped up the cap to reveal blazing deep blue eyes, darkening into purple. Almost immediately, the sergeant was in his power.

"You will bring me a pair of the best boots the army has — size eleven. And when the door closes behind me, you will come back to yourself and forget that I was ever here."

Jax left the stores and returned to HoWaRD. He entered Pedroia's office without knocking and plunked the boots down on the desk. "My mother says it's not good to cut your toenails too short."

The psychiatrist looked up in wonder. "How did you get these?"

"That information," Jax informed him, "is on a need-to-know basis."

He spun on his heel and walked out. Axel Braintree wouldn't have been proud of him. But he was pretty proud of himself.

16

When Private First Class Kevin McGuinty was summoned by his lieutenant, the young soldier's first thought was that someone had noticed the air holes in his footlocker and had discovered Augustus, the kitten he'd been keeping in the barracks.

But no, Augustus was safe for now. Instead, McGuinty was placed in front of a computer screen and told to expect a video call from "someone special."

"My mother?" McGuinty asked anxiously.

But when the caller appeared on the screen, it was the face of a preteen boy with fair hair and remarkable eyes that were . . . What color was that? A moment ago, he could have sworn they were almost as yellow as Augustus's. Yet now they were changing! Was that turquoise?

"You are very calm . . . very comfortable . . ." the caller told him.

At that moment, McGuinty knew with absolute certainty that it didn't matter what color the boy's eyes were. Everything was far too perfect to sweat small details like that.

Less than a mile away, in the northwest corner of the

post, Jax sat at his own computer. He was already deep inside the young soldier's mind. The PIP image was clear and true — his own face filling the screen of McGuinty's MacBook.

"Great," Jax approved. "Stay relaxed. When I snap my fingers, close your computer and forget everything about me and what we talked about. You'll step outside, pick a handful of clover grass, stick it in one of your socks, and put it in your footlocker."

This was the colonel's latest exercise to sharpen Jax's skills. A few times each day, he was required to bend some poor soldier via Skype and have him do something odd, so there would be proof that the suggestion had worked. Later on, a HoWaRD officer would check for the clover-filled sock in McGuinty's footlocker, or the soy sauce packet in Corporal Vanover's dress uniform pocket, or the bullet casing in the plastic bag under Sergeant Keegstra's pillow.

He was about to snap his fingers when he picked up a random impression through the mesmeric link — a tiny kitten fast asleep inside a footlocker. "Change of plan," he announced. "Instead of the footlocker, place the sock underneath your bunk." If this young soldier got some comfort out of keeping a cat hidden among his belongings, Jax didn't want to be the person who spoiled it for him.

Jax exited the video-chat program to reveal his home-page, the main screen of FreeForAll, showing all his active contacts. With a lump in his throat, he noted that Ashton

Opus was still playing Lawn Master. It was almost four hours now!

In Lawn Master, you could plant, water, fertilize, weed, cut, top-dress, spray, and aerate your virtual lawn. Dad had just spent the last four hours literally watching grass grow. It wasn't even real grass!

"There's a lot more to it than that," his father had explained. "You have to watch out for grubs. You want to get rid of them. But not the worms! You need the worms — they're natural aerators. . . ."

This from the man who used to live on the seventh floor of a luxury Manhattan high-rise. If there ever was a sign of how far the Opus family had fallen, it was Lawn Master.

Still at the computer, Jax sat back, frowning. Something felt wrong. Something . . . *hypnotic*?

Impossible. He was alone in the room. The other HoWaRDs were all busy with their own meaningless tasks. Yet there it was — the stirring in his brain, faint but unmistakable. What was going on?

The feeling vanished. Once it was gone, it was almost impossible to believe it had ever been there in the first place. Had he imagined it?

I don't think so.

Maybe he was picking up some kind of brain echo from all the other mind-benders' mesmeric activity. It had never happened before, but that didn't mean it couldn't start as his abilities continued to develop. Axel Braintree had always said there was no limit to how powerful Jax might become.

There had to be an explanation. After all, it wasn't as if a website could be hypnotic.

Could it?

Jax clicked on the white dwarf star and dragged it to the center of the blob where the nucleus would be. He regarded it with satisfaction. There. That should do it.

In the box provided to name your new constellation, he typed *Amy the Amoeba*, and gave its location in the night sky, between the Little Dipper and Draco. This was his best one yet, less ambitious than *Larry the Lamborghini*, but more complex than plain old *Iggy the iPad*, which was basically a rectangle.

Jax had discovered Constellation Factory while exploring the FreeForAll site. He was determined to identify the strange mesmeric feeling that seemed to emanate from the computer every time he logged on.

It was like trying to trap a moonbeam.

None of the other mind-benders had experienced anything like what he was describing.

"Of course, that doesn't mean it isn't happening," Dirk had reminded him. "None of us are as sensitive as you are."

"Why don't you ask Wilson?" Evelyn had suggested. "He spends more time on FreeForAll than anybody. Half the time he's 'researching,' he's playing games."

"Wilson hates it when I go on FreeForAll," Jax had replied. "It's like he has this favorite toy he refuses to share with anybody else — which is pretty stupid for a social network with two billion users."

With a sigh, Jax refocused his attention on the screen, searching for a supply of fresh stars for his next constellation.

Without warning, he was spun around in his swivel chair, winding up face-to-angry-face with Wilson.

"What are you doing, Dopus? You're supposed to be working!"

Jax bristled. "I *am* working! There's something weird coming off that site. If you'd stop picking fights with me, maybe you'd notice it, too!"

In response, Wilson gave him a mammoth shove, sending Jax rolling and whirling across the room. The chair tipped, dumping him out on the hard tile floor.

Jax scrambled up and made a beeline for his desk. Wilson stopped him halfway, lifting him up by the front of his shirt. Jax felt his feet leave the floor. He'd forgotten how strong Wilson was, and how big.

"Let go!" Jax demanded.

"Make me."

Jax boxed Wilson's ears.

"Ow!" The big boy dropped to his knees, momentarily releasing Jax.

Jax started away, but a flailing hand knocked his ankle out from under him. As he fell to the floor, he heard the voice.

Stanley's voice.

Wilson moved to stand menacingly over Jax. "I've been waiting for this a long time."

"Wilson, listen — Stanley's back!"

"What are you talking about, Dopus? Stanley's gone."

"No!" Jax insisted. "He's here! I just heard him!"

Wilson balled a fist. "You can't save yourself this time — not even by hearing voices that aren't there."

"Hey!" All at once, Captain Pedroia was on the scene, pushing them apart. "Break it up before I call the MPs!" He ducked between them, shoving Wilson away.

Wilson was outraged. "How come you're taking *his* side?"

"I'm not taking anybody's side! I'm stopping a fight between two idiots who should know better!"

Jax's mind was riveted on the voice he'd heard. "Captain — is Stanley here?"

"You know he's not," the psychiatrist snapped. "Now get up and go home. Your day is over."

"How come *he* gets the day off?" Wilson complained.

"Mind your own business!" Pedroia ordered. "What do you think the colonel would say about this?"

That was the magic word for Wilson. He idolized Brassmeyer, who had his dream job — yelling all day and pushing people around. The burly teen shuffled away, muttering under his breath.

The psychiatrist turned to Jax. "Why would you let that kid goad you into a fight? He could fracture your skull with his little finger."

"Captain, I heard Stanley. I know I did."

Pedroia regarded him critically. "You of all people know why Stanley isn't here."

Jax was adamant. "That doesn't change what I heard."

The psychiatrist frowned. "You think maybe the voice was — in your head?"

"No. In this room."

"Well, he isn't here, Jax. It's as simple as that."

Jax's eyes panned the main work area of the Hypnotic Warfare Research Department — the drab walls painted battleship gray, the beige furniture that clashed, the round table that served as their dining and break area, the various work stations, and —

His gaze landed on his own computer, its monitor still displaying the night sky of Constellation Factory. A faint connection registered in his overheated brain.

He was searching for the source of the mesmeric energy radiating from FreeForAll. Mesmeric energy came from mind-benders.

Stanley was a mind-bender.

Suddenly, he had the answer. Or, at least, a theory.

17

Monica Opus peeked around the kitchen doorway to regard her son. Jax was seated at the dining room table, where the family kept the computer. He was facing away from the screen, staring off into space, motionless, his head slightly cocked.

"What's he doing?" she whispered to her husband.

"He's hogging the computer," he replied irritably. "I need to get on there to water my lawn."

"Ashton, be serious! He's been like that for at least an hour and a half. Why would he need the computer and then sit there and ignore it?"

Jax's father frowned. "He's not ignoring it exactly. He looks like he's concentrating on something."

"Uh-oh." Mrs. Opus's eyes narrowed. "I smell hocus-pocus."

"Please don't call it that. I don't love hypnotism either. My mother bent me every time she needed someone to take out the garbage. But our son is so gifted that his own government called for his talents to help the Department of Defense. How many of us are ever that good at anything?"

"I wish he wasn't," she said fervently. "What kind of life is this for a twelve-year-old? He should be hanging out with classmates, not colonels."

Her husband nodded sadly. "We're so fixated on how miserable *we* are that we've lost sight of how hard this is on Jax."

"But that still doesn't explain what he's doing there," Mrs. Opus persisted.

"He's probably not doing anything," Mr. Opus soothed. "There's nobody here to hypnotize but us, and besides, he's facing *away* from the webcam. Chances are, he's just staring off into space while his life marches on without him. I know I've done my share of that these past few months."

"Ashton, what are we going to do? When does the time come for us to tell Colonel Brassmeyer that he's going to have to find a way to get along without our son?"

Her husband frowned. "You're forgetting Mako. Just because we can't see all this hypnotism doesn't mean the air isn't crackling with it. A construction worker killed Axel Braintree, but there's no question that Mako compelled him to do it. And we both saw him make Jax take a dive off a fifteen-story balcony. We need the army's protection."

At the dining room table, Jax was so lost in concentration that he missed his parents' urgent whispering from the kitchen. For the past hour and a half he had been listening to the background noise of Constellation Factory — futuristic electronic music mixed with bleeps and pings from outer space. It was so boring that the biggest challenge was to keep from nodding off in his chair.

But this was the site that had been giving off strange mesmeric energy. It was also the site that had been open when Jax had heard Stanley's voice during the brawl with Wilson. Those two facts had to be connected. And Jax had a theory that might explain everything.

Everyone believed that Jax was the only mind-bender who could hypnotize remotely. What if someone else could do it, too — someone like Stanley? The kid was powerful enough. Jax was Opus and Sparks, but Stanley was Arcanov. And Stanley had bent Jax one-on-one at HoWaRD that time.

The theory was this: A hypnotic message from Stanley was going out over FreeForAll. That's what Jax had over-heard while he'd been wrestling with Wilson. And why hadn't he noticed the message during his many hours playing Constellation Factory? The answer came from his own role in Operation Aurora. At the end of the video clip, he had commanded his viewers to forget ever having seen or heard him. Surely Stanley would be using the same order — *and Stanley was capable of hypnotizing Jax!*

Jax hadn't *missed* Stanley's message on FreeForAll. He'd probably heard it dozens of times. But he'd been bent and instructed to forget it.

There was only one way to prove this crazy hypothesis. He had to sit here — facing away from the screen — until the message came up again. If he could hear it *without* seeing it and becoming hypnotized, he'd be able to remember it.

His father emerged from the kitchen to stand over him. "Penny for your thoughts, kid?"

"Hi, Dad."

"Any chance of me getting on the machine?" Ashton Opus grinned sheepishly. "My grass is dying as we speak."

Lawn Master was a FreeForAll game, just like Constellation Factory. If, as Jax suspected, Stanley's hypnotic message was being distributed via the entire site, it should come up anywhere on FreeForAll.

"Sure, Dad. Knock yourself out."

He relinquished the seat, and leaned against the side of the table, careful to keep his eyes averted from the monitor.

"Will you look at that!" complained Mr. Opus as his virtual lawn appeared. "It's turning brown already! And is that *crab grass*?"

"At least there are no dandelions," Jax soothed.

"What I really need is Weed-n-Feed, but I don't have enough coins. Hmmm, the Lawn Doctor pack is nine ninety-nine, but I can upgrade to Greens-Keeper level for another five bucks. . . ." His voice trailed off.

Jax waited for more. His father was focused on the screen with a fierce intensity.

A child's voice came out of the speakers. "Look into my eyes. . . ."

Stanley!

Jax whipped his phone out of his pocket. It was

already set to the microphone app. Breathlessly, he tapped RECORD.

"You are very relaxed. . . . Everything is wonderful, and you're happy to listen to what I have to say. In a few seconds, I'll clap my hands, and you'll remember nothing of me or this message. You'll go back to your regular routine — until Wednesday, October Twenty-Fourth, at nine AM *Eastern time. That's six* AM *Pacific, two* PM *Greenwich Mean, ten* PM *in Japan. Take a moment to think about what time this will be for you. . . . At that moment, you will stop what you're doing and remain motionless. It is incredibly urgent that you do this exactly the way I've described it. . . ."*

Jax listened in growing horror. It was Operation Aurora all over again! But this time it wasn't happening in one isolated test town in the middle of the desert. FreeForAll was the most popular site on the web, with users in the billions. This was going worldwide! Why else would Stanley make such a big deal of getting the time zones right?

How could Brassmeyer be so crazy? They saw what happened in Delta Prime! It was a total meltdown! Who could guess how many people would have died if helicopters hadn't been standing by to pluck out the injured and fly them to medical attention?

But there weren't enough helicopters on earth to respond to an Operation Aurora that was happening everywhere at the same time!

It would be nothing less than a catastrophe on a global scale.

"You will stay perfectly still," Stanley's voice continued, *"until you hear this special word — the name of what I'm holding in my hand right now. Remember it well . . ."*

Jax was torn in two. He had to see what the boy was holding. But the instant he looked, he'd be in danger of being hypnotized and forgetting everything he'd just heard. And then he'd be unable to sound the alarm.

"You will have no memory of what I've told you." The sound of Stanley's clap made Jax jump.

Mr. Opus blinked as he came out of his mesmeric trance.

"Dad," Jax ventured tentatively, "do you remember what you just saw?"

"Of course," his father replied. "The Greens-Keeper pack is a better deal. You get triple the coins, *plus* Weed-n-Feed. . . ."

Jax's heart sank. Before his very eyes, he'd watched Dad fall victim to this Super Aurora. He fought off the impulse to hypnotize his father himself and try to undo the damage. Once planted, a post-hypnotic suggestion was virtually impossible to counteract. Besides, Stanley's message was running constantly. A FreeForAll fanatic like Ashton Opus would be bent and re-bent dozens of times in the coming weeks, along with millions of others. Who knew how many had already been implanted with the post-hypnotic suggestion? If this continued on the world's top website, by October 24, *billions* could be impacted. And the destruction and loss of life — he thought back to little Delta Prime. It was beyond imagining.

He shuddered with a surge of anger toward Colonel Brassmeyer. And Captain Pedroia, too. The psychiatrist had told him that Stanley had been *adopted*, knowing full well that the eight-year-old had been removed from the rest of HoWaRD in order to lead this horrific experiment!

And how gullible was I to believe it?

Jax felt himself reddening with shame. He'd actually considered Pedroia a nice guy. Now he realized the psychiatrist was no different than Brassmeyer or any of those military types — ruthless, single-minded robots programmed to do anything to complete the mission, no matter what the cost.

I ought to take my size-eleven boots back!

But a pair of boots, or catching someone in a lie, meant little compared with the huge cataclysm the Hypnotic Warfare Research Department was about to unleash on an unsuspecting world. Jax had to stop it.

But how?

18

Colonel Brassmeyer's aide was gone for the day, so the outer office was deserted.

Jax kicked open the inner door and barked, "What do you think you're doing?"

The colonel didn't glance up from some papers he was examining. "What now, Opus?"

"It's another Aurora, isn't it?" Jax accused. "With Stanley this time."

"You don't know what you're talking about. Stanley's gone —"

"From here maybe!" Jax cut him off. "You moved him someplace safe, because this time your little experiment is going to trash the world, not just a fake town!"

Now Brassmeyer did look up, his face a mixture of anger and concern. "I'm not sure where you got this crazy idea, Opus, but you're way out of line. What are you talking about?"

In answer, Jax tapped the PLAY button on his phone. *"You are very relaxed,"* came Stanley's voice. *"Everything is wonderful, and you're happy to listen to what I have to say. . . ."*

Brassmeyer sat forward in his chair, listening intently as the message played out. "Where did you get that?"

"Like you don't know," Jax shot back. "It's on FreeForAll, playing over and over, reaching two billion users. Come October Twenty-Fourth, what happened in Delta Prime is going to happen worldwide — and this time you won't be able to control it with a few helicopters and a field hospital. Why would you do such a terrible thing? Did the army order you to do it? Does the president know?"

For the first time, Brassmeyer's voice was deathly quiet. "Sit down and shut up."

Jax was too agitated to sit, but he folded his arms in front of him to await the explanation that surely must be coming.

"I can't tell you what the president knows. He doesn't give orders to me. He doesn't even give orders to the guy who *does* give orders to me. There are a lot of levels between the president and me. It's called a chain of command, and it's something that you're completely incapable of figuring out. Maybe it's your fancy New York upbringing, but for some reason you think you're always entitled to ask the question *why?* In the army that's the one question that is none of your business. You take orders, you give orders, you follow orders. That's all there is."

Jax opened his mouth to protest, but Brassmeyer held up his hand. "Just this once, I'm going to answer your big fat *why*. It's a hoax."

"I heard it with my own ears," Jax persisted. "My dad got bent by it."

"Unleashing that message on a global scale isn't an exercise, it's a doomsday machine," the colonel insisted. "Nobody's crazy enough to do that! That's what operations like Aurora are all about — to see what a weapon is capable of and analyze the consequences of using it. Think logically! How does the army benefit from wrecking the world? We'd be destroying ourselves, too."

"If the army isn't doing it," Jax challenged, "then who is?"

"That's what I'm telling you. *Nobody* is."

Jax waved his phone in Brassmeyer's face. "Then what's this recording? That's Stanley's voice!"

The colonel shook his head. "It's a kid's voice, I'll grant you that. But it can't be Stanley. He's out of the picture. Besides, you have no evidence that he's capable of the kind of remote hypnotism you are."

"Is he?" Jax probed.

"That's classified."

"I have all the evidence I need — the fact that he did it! I've got it on tape! What more do you need? The only thing I don't have is the trigger word to turn it all off. I couldn't see what he was holding without looking at the screen and getting bent myself!"

Brassmeyer picked up the phone. "I'm calling Pedroia. You may be *my* problem, but the fact that you're losing it is *his* problem."

Jax's mind raced. If he let this call go through, the

psychiatrist would be there soon. As long as Jax was still one-on-one with the colonel, he had an advantage.

He opened his eyes wide for maximum power and turned them on Brassmeyer. The colonel reached to clamp a hand over Jax's face, letting go of the receiver, which clattered to the desktop. Jax backed away just a step, keeping his mesmerizing stare trained on his opponent.

Brassmeyer turned his face aside. "You're making a big mistake!" he gasped.

Jax lunged to get himself back into his subject's line of sight, but the colonel kept his eyes averted. Determined to regain his attention, Jax snatched a vase off a shelf and smashed it to the floor. It broke into a million pieces. Involuntarily, Brassmeyer wheeled in the direction of the sound of shattering pottery. Jax was in position to intercept his gaze. For a moment, the PIP was right there — himself as the colonel saw him. Then the image swung away as Brassmeyer nearly broke his neck to avoid Jax's hypnotic assault. Jax could see his face mirrored in the glass of the framed West Point diploma on the wall.

How am I going to get him? Jax thought desperately. *All he has to do is keep staring at that diploma!*

And then he had the answer. He focused in on his subject's image in the glass and shuffled forward until their eyes locked. And there, through the reflection, the mesmeric link was formed.

The connection was slow and weak, and when the PIP

reappeared, it showed Jax's face in the glass of the frame, his eyes dark and luminous, but not any distinct color. He felt like the hypnotic equivalent of a lion tamer, trying to control a powerful and unpredictable beast through feeble, unreliable means.

"That's it," Jax said nervously. "No reason to be so angry. . . . Everything is going your way, and you're very calm. . . ." He almost giggled. *Calm* was a word that could never be used to describe this man. "Now relax. . . . All is well. . . . Have a seat."

The PIP image vanished for a moment as the colonel all but collapsed into his chair. Jax hurriedly sat on the edge of the desk and reestablished eye contact. The connection was stronger now, and Jax's comfort level grew.

"You have to believe what I tell you because it's true." Now that he was sure that the army was not behind Stanley's message, it was urgent to convince the colonel that the danger was real. "Someone is using Stanley X to create a ginormous Operation Aurora that will affect the whole world. This is the greatest threat that you have ever faced as an army officer. Nothing else even comes close. Do you understand?"

"Acknowledged." Bent or not, he was all military.

"So what do we do?" Jax asked urgently.

"Stanley has become an unacceptable threat. Threats must be neutralized," Brassmeyer replied immediately.

"How?" Jax persisted.

"Targeted assassination."

"No!" It was like a blow to the stomach. "I mean — uh — isn't there a less drastic way to handle it? He's just a kid."

"Mesmeric power is a military asset but also a potential danger, as human nature is impossible to control. The only fail-safe way to contain a rogue mind-bender is to eliminate him altogether."

It was an automatic reply that sent a chill down Jax's spine. The way Brassmeyer recited it made it clear that this was not just a spur-of-the-moment response. It was policy — and it would apply to every single one of them. If Jax, and not Stanley, were the threat here, *he* would be the one in the crosshairs.

I should have known!

Of course the army had a plan for what to do to hypnotists who went off the rails. The army had a plan for everything. While HoWaRD was welcoming them to use their powers to serve their country, there was a contingency in place to eliminate them if those same powers ever got out of hand.

"Okay," he said in a small voice. "Scratch that. You will forget everything I just told you about Stanley. You will leave Stanley alone." His heart was racing. This didn't solve the problem of the global Aurora that was coming.

He had a flash of inspiration. "Tell me everything you know about the people who adopted Stanley."

Instantly, Jax sensed a change in the colonel's attitude. A prolonged mesmeric link conveyed more than words and images. It was a connection of two minds — a sharing of emotion and personality. Brassmeyer was a hard man. His no-nonsense toughness came through every bit as clearly as the picture-in-picture image of what he saw. Yet as soon as Jax mentioned Stanley's adoption, a warmth and even joy began to leach through the mental conduit.

"His name is Ferguson," Brassmeyer replied. "A family man, a good man. He was so happy to have found the child of his long-lost cousin. . . ."

As his subject droned on about the details surrounding Stanley's adoptive father, Jax marveled at the colonel's transformation. Rather than reluctance to give up HoWaRD's number-two mind-bender, all Jax saw was pure happiness that the young orphan had found such an ideal home. Jax was especially amazed that the normally impatient Brassmeyer had taken the time and effort to research the Fergusons to make sure that Stanley was bound for the best possible situation that any child could hope for.

The colonel went on and on about the specifics of the adoption, painting such a vivid picture that a memory began to seep through the link, reforming itself as a diorama in Jax's mind. It was the courtroom on the day of the hearing. Everyone was smiling — the judge, the lawyers, the social workers. Jax couldn't see Brassmeyer, since the memory was through his eyes. But he could feel the man's happiness and serenity.

Stanley was smiling, too, if a little nervously, as he headed off to his new life with his new dad.

The courtroom and its inhabitants faded out as Jax focused in on Mr. Ferguson. He was tall, with a shock of dark hair, a hawklike nose, and black, black eyes under striking brows.

He was Dr. Elias Mako.

19

The office tilted and went a little gray for a moment. Jax slipped off the edge of the desk and was lucky to find his chair. Otherwise, he would have had to pick himself up off the floor, and he couldn't be sure that enough strength remained in his arms and legs to accomplish that.

Brassmeyer's PIP flickered, and Jax struggled back onto the desktop to maintain eye contact. The last thing he needed was for the colonel to come back to himself now — before he'd been commanded to forget all this.

"In a moment, you're going to wake up," Jax told his subject, "but *not* before you hear your office door click shut. I wasn't here. No one was here. You were alone the whole time, and you're not mad at me at all, not about anything."

He fled, grateful that the colonel's aide had not returned. Jax didn't stop running as he left the building and started across the post toward home.

Mako! The plot was so insane that Jax could barely wrap his mind around it to connect the far-flung dots. No wonder a crab like Brassmeyer was so giddy with happiness over Stanley's "adoption." No wonder he'd given up an important asset without an argument. He'd been hypnotized by the master. He could just as easily have been made to believe that Fort Calhoun was a cheerleading camp and, as soon as he found his pom-poms, he was going out there to lead the Green Berets in their new human pyramid. Mako was just that good.

The colonel had been right about one thing, though. The army would never be crazy enough to try a global Aurora. That kind of evil took a madman like Mako.

Somehow — *through Wilson?* — Mako must have found out about Stanley and his growing powers. He realized Jax would never cooperate with him again. But now there was a new rising star, an Arcanov, even younger and more easily manipulated. Knowing Stanley was an orphan, all Mako had to do was impersonate a long-lost relative. Anybody who asked questions — like Colonel Brassmeyer, or a lawyer, or a judge — could simply be bent.

It all made sense! Mako, who had nurtured Jax's talent for remote hypnotism, had coaxed the same ability out of Stanley. And his terrible plan had come straight from the army's own playbook for Operation Aurora — with a twist.

This new Aurora would not be restricted to an isolated, controlled environment like Delta Prime. Anybody anywhere could suddenly stop dead at the appointed hour on October 24 — pilots flying planeloads of passengers, engineers running nuclear power stations, presidents and prime ministers charged with the safety of entire nations, mountain climbers leading expeditions on high peaks.

Trains, buses, and cars would careen out of control, fires would start and spread, vital infrastructure would be destroyed. Those unaffected by the post-hypnotic suggestion would be in a panic. Even those who remained calm would be powerless to save the rest as roads clogged and cities ground to a halt. The casualties would be unimaginable.

And Mako alone would control the trigger word that could put a stop to it. Even Jax, who knew what was going on, didn't dare risk trying to glimpse what Stanley held in his hand in the hypnotic message. It was classic Mako — as brilliant as it was twisted.

He entered their cottage breathless and sweat-soaked. Dad was still playing Lawn Master. There was no question that Stanley's message had reached him countless times. Probably Mom, too, just by living in the same house and having nothing to do but fiddle with the computer. This would be far more than a tragedy involving nameless, faceless strangers. This had found his own parents in their tiny corner of the world.

At that moment, he felt the absence of Axel Braintree as a raw open wound. Axel would know what to do. He had devoted his life to fighting the unethical use of hypnotic power — whether it was one of his sandmen bending a hot-dog vendor for a free lunch or Mako trying to rig a presidential election. Axel had seen through Mako and opposed him right from the start.

But Axel's gone. I'm the only one who knows Mako's plans.

Who could he tell? Brassmeyer? The colonel had already dismissed the recording as a hoax. And not even hypnotism could convince him that Stanley was in the hands of an evil man — not after Brassmeyer had been bent by Mako first. Pedroia? He'd have to go through the colonel, chain of command and all that. The police? He'd be starting at square one, trying to convince them that such hypnotism even existed.

He ran into his room and threw himself down on the bed. What about a second video clip? He could record it himself, try to override Stanley's post-hypnotic suggestion. Hypnotism didn't usually work that way, but shouldn't he at least try?

With a sinking heart, he realized that wasn't an option either. Even if he could craft the perfect mesmeric message, how would he distribute it? Stanley's video was all over a website with two billion users. Jax could never hope to reach even a tiny fraction of that — not with the clock ticking down.

There was no way for Jax to stop this global meltdown. Despite the combined power of Opus and Sparks, he would be nothing but a spectator for the coming horror show. Everybody in the world would be — except Mako and his adopted "son," Stanley.

An awful thought struck Jax. What hypnotic blowback must that eight-year-old kid be suffering? The seven hundred fifty-three inhabitants of little Delta Prime had put Jax flat on his back. What must it be like to get the mental backwash of the entire world? Could poor Stanley stand upright, walk, talk, think? Was he even alive? Certainly Elias Mako wouldn't think twice about sacrificing the life of a child in order to achieve his hideous goals.

Jax set his jaw, suddenly sure of his only possible course of action. He would find Mako and Stanley and force them to stop this looming catastrophe.

Instantly, a laundry list of reasons why this was impossible appeared in Jax's mind. He would have to sneak away from Fort Calhoun and abandon his parents. He was looking for someone who was probably in hiding, and he had absolutely no idea where. He'd have to hypnotize Mako, something he had never been able to do before. He wasn't even sure that he could handle Stanley, who was the only hypnotist alive besides Mako who had succeeded in bending Jax.

He shook his head to clear it. If he'd had any choice other than sitting around waiting for the world to end, he would have jumped at it.

But there was no other choice. He had to go, and he had to go now.

The question remained: Where would you look for somebody if you had absolutely no idea where to start?

Thanks to the escape from prison, Mako's trail had gone cold. The last place it could be picked up was at his Sentia Institute in Jax's hometown.

New York City.

20

"Dad." Jax shook his father's shoulder gently. "I need you to wake up for a second."

Ashton Opus rolled over in bed. "What time is it?"

Jax switched on the small lamp on the nightstand. "It's after one. Can you see me?"

With great effort, Dad forced his eyes open, blinking away sleep. "What is it, kid? Something wrong?"

Jax waited for his father to focus on him, and then said, "Nothing is wrong. . . . Everything is fine. . . . You are very relaxed. . . ."

The picture-in-picture image appeared, blurry from interrupted sleep, yet otherwise strong — himself, leaning over the bed, his eyes blazing deep amethyst. He regretted bending Mom and Dad after he'd promised not to, but it was for their own good.

Besides, there was so much to be regretted these days that a little bonus hypnotism was the least of their worries.

"You'll be asleep again in just a minute," Jax went on soothingly. "When you wake up in the morning, I'll be gone. But you have to ignore whatever you hear about me. Remember only this: I'm fine. There's no reason for you and Mom to come looking for me. Stay here at Fort Calhoun and let the army continue to protect you. That's the most important thing."

With a heavy heart, he tiptoed out of the bedroom and past his mother, who had fallen asleep in front of the TV. Five minutes before, he had given her the same mesmeric pep talk, and she had promised not to worry. She would, of course; they both would. But there was nothing Jax could do about that. It was one of the limitations of hypnotism. You could order someone to change a lightbulb or bake cookies. But you couldn't tell them how they were going to feel about it. He had blazed a trail in their minds that would lead them to conclude that he was okay. But there was no way he could command them to follow it when everything in their hearts told them the opposite.

And anyway, why should they believe him when he didn't even believe himself? He had instructed his parents not to worry, but in reality, he had no idea if he would ever lay eyes on them again.

He hefted his backpack, appalled by how light it was. He was walking away from his entire life with nothing but a cell phone and a single change of clothing. He had a grand total of thirty dollars and forty-four cents, which he knew wouldn't take him very far. His only other asset was his color-changing eyes, which he knew could get him anywhere he wanted to go.

An army post like Fort Calhoun was never completely deserted, even at one thirty in the morning. Soon, a Jeep sidled up.

"I'll need to see some ID, soldier," called a uniformed MP. A flashlight beam played over Jax. "Whoa, isn't this a little past your bedtime, kid?" He peered into Jax's downcast face.

It was a mistake. Jax raised his head to turn his eyes on the corporal, and the man was lost.

"Look into my eyes," Jax commanded when the PIP appeared. "Now train your light on my collar. Two shiny stars gleam back at you."

"General!" The corporal snapped a salute, bobbling and dropping his flashlight. It hit the floor of the Jeep and went out. "I'm sorry, sir. We weren't told —"

"Uh — at ease, son." It was the rare case when a military order might actually be stronger than a hypnotic one. In the army, a general trumped everything and everybody.

"I need you to drive me to the bus station in Lawton," Jax went on. He would get to New York more quickly by air, but military planes were tracked, and airports were crowded places. Jax couldn't depend on being able to bend so many people at the same time.

The bus, then. At any given time, there were thousands of buses on the move around the country, and nobody kept track of who was on them. Getting to New York the slow way was better than running the risk that he wouldn't get there at all.

"Hop in, General," the MP invited.

At the main gate, the sentry leaned out of the booth. "Who's your passenger?"

"I'm just taking the general into Lawton," came the reply.

"The *general*?" The sentry gaped at the twelve-year-old in the other seat.

Jax caught the sentry's eyes with a single scorching stare. "You will let us pass, and forget you ever saw us or this Jeep. . . . It's a quiet night, and nobody's been through this gate for hours."

When the barrier lifted, he turned to his driver. "Let's get a move on, son. I'm not getting any younger."

As they roared down the road, Jax peered over his shoulder at the sleeping Fort Calhoun. He'd never wanted to go there, had hated pretty much everything about the place. But right then it seemed like the closest thing he had to a home.

Ahead lay only uncertainty.

———————————

In Fort Calhoun's motor pool, Staff Sergeant Chen frowned at the clock. All the MPs on the first night watch had checked in — all but Corporal Gordon. Where was he? The shift had ended almost an hour ago! He'd been hailing him via walkie-talkie for the past twenty minutes. If Gordon was dodging his calls . . .

He picked up the phone and dialed the gatehouse. "It's Chen in the motor pool. What time did Corporal Gordon pass there?"

"He didn't," droned the reply. "It's a quiet night, and nobody's passed through this gate for hours."

Chen had no way of knowing that the sentry was responding to a hypnotic command, yet something in his tone of voice didn't seem right to the experienced motor-pool chief. He jumped in a Jeep and retraced the MP's route around the post. He saw the personnel from the second shift. But there was no sign of Gordon and his vehicle.

Dumb kid was probably asleep in a grove of trees somewhere off the beaten path. But just in case . . .

He took out his cell phone and dialed a number. "I've got a possible code two-four, missing Jeep." As an after-thought, he added, "And a missing MP with it." As the motor-pool chief, only the vehicle was his responsibility, but it couldn't hurt to mention Gordon, too.

The alert would establish roadblocks along the major routes in and out of Fort Calhoun. It was probably a false alarm, but he had to follow protocol. At least it would teach Gordon a lesson about turning in his Jeep on schedule.

21

Corporal Gordon was making excellent time because the general had authorized him to exceed the speed limit.

About thirty miles east of Fort Calhoun, they rounded a bend and came up behind a long line of stopped cars and trucks.

A traffic jam? Jax thought in dismay. *At two in the morning?*

He spied the red-and-blue flashers of police cruisers. Silhouetted against the headlights, officers in broad-brimmed hats peered into windows.

A roadblock!

"Kill your headlights!" he rasped urgently.

"Sir?" queried the corporal.

"Do it now!" Jax looked around urgently. To their right, a wall of cornstalks rose just beyond the highway. "Drive into that field. That's an order!"

Gordon wrenched the steering wheel. They left the road, hurtled over the ditch, and plowed into the tall stalks. On they jounced, totally blind, the corn plants swinging back and battering them as the Jeep smashed its way through.

"Stop!" Jax commanded, almost smothered.

Gordon slammed on the brakes and the vehicle shuddered to a halt in the shelter of the plants.

"What now, General?" the MP asked breathlessly.

"I'm thinking!" Jax took stock of his situation. If they went forward, they'd be caught and dragged back to Brassmeyer. But turning around wasn't an option either. To find an alternate route on these tiny rural highways would be virtually impossible — and there was no guarantee that there weren't roadblocks on all of them.

He turned to Gordon, who was sitting passively in the driver's seat, awaiting instructions. In spite of everything else, Jax felt a wave of guilt. This young MP was AWOL with army property, thirty miles away from where he was supposed to be. All on the orders of a general who didn't really exist. The guy was in big trouble, and it was Jax's fault.

"Listen carefully, soldier, and do exactly what I tell you. Turn this Jeep around, and drive straight back to Fort Calhoun. When they stop you at the gate, tell them you have a message, but you can only give it to Colonel Brassmeyer. Here's the message: 'Jackson Opus says hi.'" It wasn't an in-your-face to the colonel. Brassmeyer was the only senior officer on the post who would understand that the young MP had been hypnotized, and was not at fault.

Jax jumped out of the Jeep to stand amid the corn.

Gordon regarded him in concern. "Are you sure you're going to be okay, sir?"

Jax allowed himself a hint of a smile. "Don't worry. We generals are — um — always okay."

The corporal snapped a salute that Jax returned. The Jeep wheeled around, bulldozed a path through the corn, and thumped back onto the pavement.

Jax backtracked toward the highway, but remained hidden among the high plants. He began to bushwhack parallel to the road. Soon he'd reached the end of the line of stopped vehicles — mostly trucks at this late hour. Up ahead, two state troopers were shining flashlights into windshields. Seeds of a new plan took hold in Jax's mind. The bus station in Lawton was out. But these were big rigs carrying cargo all across the country. Surely in all that rolling stock there had to be a place for one twelve-year-old to hide.

Peering out from between two stalks, he made sure the troopers' attention was focused elsewhere. The coast was clear.

Jax leaped the ditch and dashed to the back of an eighteen-wheel rig. He jumped onto the steel step and grabbed the latch to open the double doors.

Oh, no! Locked!

Heart pounding faster now, he scampered along the side of the trailer up to the truck ahead of it. This one had a single roll-up door. The padlock was roughly the size of his head.

Panicking a little, he tried to picture the length of the queue. He was still pretty far back, but sooner or later, someone was bound to notice a crazed kid dashing from semi to semi.

Third from the back was a green trailer marked FREIGHT UNLIMITED. His heart sank. Another padlock. But wait — the long silver hasp wasn't completely closed. Jackpot!

He raised the door just high enough that he could roll himself inside. When the gate rattled shut behind him, the blackness was absolutely total. He couldn't even see his own hand in front of his face.

I might as well be in deep space, minus the stars.

He fumbled for his phone, whispering aloud, "Don't drop it . . . don't drop it . . . don't drop it." The device would be his only source of light in this suffocating black. If he lost it, he would never find it again.

When the screen lit up, his sense of relief almost brought tears to his eyes. He activated the flashlight app and explored his surroundings. The truck's payload was stacked high with hundreds of cartons piled on wooden skids. The boxes were unmarked except for a stamp: FOODSTUFFS. Well, at least he wouldn't starve in here. There was something to eat. He devoutly hoped it wasn't Brussels sprouts. Axel Braintree had once scolded Jax for trying to implant Mom with a post-hypnotic suggestion that Brussels sprouts could only be eaten in Belgium.

The thought of his mother brought a lump to his throat. In a few hours, she and Dad would be waking up to the fact that he was gone.

He squeezed behind a skid, moved a stack of boxes, and made a hiding place for himself. If the troopers opened the payload, at least they wouldn't see him outright.

They'd have to search the whole truck to find him. He was reasonably sure they wouldn't do that.

For the next five minutes or so, the semi inched forward in start-and-stop motion. Jax knew they were making their way to the roadblock itself, but the effect on an unofficial passenger was stomach-churning. At last, they must have been waved through because the engine roared louder and the vehicle began to pick up speed. Jax stepped out of his hiding place, relieved that this first hurdle had been cleared.

The next order of business was to get himself to New York. But since he couldn't exactly climb out of a speeding truck, he had to wait until the driver made a pit stop somewhere. In the meantime, keeping his strength up was priority one. It was time to learn what "foodstuffs" meant.

He tore into one of the cartons. Inside he found one hundred forty-four individual packets of Skittles. It managed to restore a little of his mood. No, not Brussels sprouts — candy. Without hesitation, he banged down eight small bags. Mom might find this even more disturbing than the fact that he was going to New York in the first place. It was a seriously unbalanced breakfast, but the sugar would keep him awake and alert. In fact, after a few minutes, it was all he could do to keep himself from bouncing off the sides of the trailer.

In spite of it all, he actually managed to doze a little. In the end, it was the truck noise that brought him back to life — the big motor grinding as the Skittle-mobile geared down, veering onto an off ramp. Jax could feel the vehicle slowing, and he noticed something else, too. Light was entering the payload via cracks at the side of the gate. It was morning, and the driver was probably stopping for breakfast.

Good. Jax had to meet this man face-to-face.

The huge tires crunched to a halt and the big engine fell silent. A moment later, Jax heard the slam of the cab door.

He reached down to throw open the gate and nearly pulled every muscle in his back. For some reason, the heavy door was a lot harder to move from the inside. At last, he raised it just enough to squeeze out. He hit the pavement running and identified his driver en route to the restaurant of a large truck stop. Black-and-red-checked jacket — that was him.

Oops — her. So much for his plan to hypnotize her in the bathroom.

Well, he would just have to try to do it out in the open. Luckily, people didn't usually notice what they didn't expect to see — like a twelve-year-old bending a lady trucker at a rest stop.

He caught up with her at the lunch counter and took the stool beside hers. "Coffee, huh?"

"Yep. Can't be too hot or too strong." She turned to smile at him and he froze her with blazing eyes.

"You're enjoying your coffee, and when your breakfast comes, it will be delicious, too. When you pay your bill, you will forget this conversation. All you will remember is that the final destination for your cargo is New York City."

For an instant, the PIP image — himself from her perspective — flickered. A hint of rebellion, perhaps. She frowned and said uncertainly, "Erie, Pennsylvania."

Jax felt a stirring of respect for this trucker's devotion to her schedule and cargo. But this was no time to give in. "New York," he repeated firmly. "Manhattan. Look into my eyes. You can read it on your manifest. New York City. They love Skittles in New York."

"New York City," she echoed.

"Good," Jax approved. "You'll be driving alone. It might look like I'll be in the passenger seat beside you. But I'm not there."

"I drive alone," she droned.

The waitress behind the counter approached Jax. "What can I get you, hon?"

"Burger and fries to go." He considered adding "Put it on her tab," but for some reason, that didn't seem right.

Funny, he reflected. He had no problem taking her and her shipment of Skittles to the wrong city. But he couldn't bring himself to stick her with his tab.

22

New York.

It was after one AM, but the instant the familiar skyline appeared across the dark Hudson River, Jax knew the emotion of coming home.

"You want to take the Holland Tunnel," he said almost automatically. "There's always night construction at the Lincoln this time of year."

The driver didn't hear him. He was, after all, not there. He waited until the semi was safely stopped in traffic, then bent her again. "Your destination is in lower Manhattan, east side," he instructed, giving the address.

With a grinding of gears, the truck headed into the tunnel. Jax wasn't sure why he'd chosen this particular endpoint. Mostly, he couldn't think of any other place to go. The Sandman's Guild had fallen apart after Axel's death, so there was no point in visiting their old meeting place, the Laundromat. And Mako's Sentia Institute had shut down when its founder had gone to prison. Now that he was a fugitive, Mako wasn't likely to be hanging out at his old headquarters.

Fugitive. The word reverberated in Jax's brain. *I'm a*

fugitive, too — from the US Army. Colonel Brassmeyer wasn't going to let him go just like that. Jax knew too much about HoWaRD and the military's development of hypnotic warfare.

Jax had no home in this city anymore — not since his family had fled Dr. Mako many months before. He had no apartment here, no life. Only one connection still remained, the person he'd always been able to count on.

At last, the familiar block appeared in the front window of the semi. Jax had never loved this row of low walk-up apartment buildings before, but, oh, how he loved it now. The neighborhood was a beautiful sight, unremarkable as it was in this city of towering skyscrapers.

"This is where I get off," he told the driver. "Don't get used to it. You're going to forget it in a minute. Change of plan — your new destination is your old destination in Erie, Pennsylvania. It's on your GPS. Sorry to take you out of your way. Good thing Skittles don't go bad."

Standing on the sidewalk, he watched the truck disappear around the corner, and hoped the driver could find her way all right. Then he walked into the shadowy alley and stopped behind the third building in from the avenue.

The wrought iron fire escape was in the "up" position, which meant that the ladder was completely out of reach. Even balanced atop a garbage can, his grasping fingers were well below the bottom rung.

Well, he hadn't escaped the army and come all the way from Oklahoma to be turned away because the stupid ladder was too high. He was a New Yorker, and New Yorkers knew how to make things happen.

Two garbage cans, then. Plus a third to use to climb to the top of the two. Teetering dangerously at the summit of his creation, he experienced a moment of dread as he contemplated the impact of his skull on the concrete of the alley.

Don't think about it.

He leaped and felt his hands close on the bottom rung. He'd done it!

His triumph was instantly replaced by dismay as his weight pulled the ladder all the way to the "down" position with an ear-splitting screech of ancient iron. At the bottom, his flailing feet kicked over his structure of garbage cans. In the quiet of the night, the racket seemed twice as loud, echoing off the brick walls. He fully expected half the city to descend on this disturber of the peace. Instead, not a single voice protested his presence. That was another thing about New Yorkers: It took a lot to get their attention.

Once on the fire escape, he paused only to raise the ladder back into place. It was an easy climb to the third floor. He could see through the opening in the curtains — the familiar movie posters, the beanbag chair held together with duct tape, the Eli Manning bobblehead.

He knocked on the window, timidly at first, then louder. The dark tousled head on the pillow stirred, although the sleeper did not awaken.

He shrugged out of his backpack and rapped the buckle against the glass.

It did the trick. Tommy Cicerelli sat bolt upright and stared at the figure at his window. His mouth formed one word: *Opus?*

Jax grinned in spite of himself. He hadn't been sure Tommy would even recognize him. Jax's last act before leaving New York had been to hypnotize Tommy and make him forget that the two of them had been anything more than casual acquaintances. It had been for Tommy's own protection — Mako wouldn't care who he had to chew up and spit out in order to get to Jax. Still, it was one of the saddest things Jax had ever been forced to do.

Tommy opened the window a crack, staring in confused recognition. "What are you doing here?"

Jax bit his lip to stifle his rising emotion. "How's it going, Tommy?"

Tommy blinked the sleep out of his eyes. "You *disappeared*, man! Nobody had any idea what happened to you!"

Jax was caught off guard. "I had to get out of town suddenly," he managed. "It was a family thing. Can I please come in? I've had a long trip."

Tommy opened the window and helped him inside, but his agitation only seemed to grow. "You were *missing*! It was like one day you were here, and the next —"

Jax watched in amazement as two big tears spilled out of Tommy's dark eyes and rolled down his cheeks. Why was Tommy so upset about this? Had something gone wrong with the post-hypnotic suggestion? He was way too emotionally involved over the random classmate Jax was supposed to be. Jax had been absolutely clear about that. His exact words had been: *You and Jackson Opus were never very close. It really doesn't bother you that he's not around anymore.*

Tommy was embarrassed. "I'm sorry, man. I hardly know you. But for some reason, I thought maybe you were, like, *dead* —"

Standing in the darkness of one forty-five AM, Jax felt a surge of warmth toward this boy who had been his best friend since kindergarten. Yes, you could use hypnotism to change the details of their relationship in his memory. But the attachment and the loyalty were both still there. It was comforting to know that mesmerism — as powerful as it was — couldn't wipe away everything. Not even the combined powers of Opus and Sparks could make a stranger out of the world's greatest friend.

But Tommy was entitled to remember the whole thing. He deserved the truth.

Jax fixed him with a double-barreled stare. It wasn't easy to bend Tommy. The kid was color-blind, and therefore incapable of seeing Jax's eyes change color. Tommy's world was black and white, with shades of gray.

"What's going on, Opus? What are you doing?"

"Look into my eyes!" Jax commanded.

"I am. It's getting weird."

"Concentrate, Tommy!" Jax stared harder. Color-blind or no, he had bent the guy before, and he could do it again. Especially now, with the benefit of training from Axel Braintree and the United States Department of Defense.

Finally, the PIP image began to appear. Jax knew it had to be Tommy, since it was like an old black-and-white movie. Jax's eyes, normally a sunburst of color, swirled with gray smoke.

"It's coming back to you," Jax told him. It was normally complicated to undo a previous mesmeric command, but Tommy sort of remembered anyway — the emotion, if not the specifics. "All our history together. Except maybe that love poem to Amy Biltmore in fifth grade. You can keep on forgetting about that. I wish I could. I'm going to snap my fingers now, and you'll wake up."

Tommy blinked three times. When he returned to himself, his first impulse was anger.

"How could you do that to me?" he raged, shoving Jax backward into the beanbag.

"Shhh! You'll wake your folks!"

"You jerk! What would make you disappear without so much as a good-bye?"

"Think, Tommy! Remember Dr. Mako?" Step by step, Jax brought his friend up to speed on why the Opus family had run away from New York, and these last few months at Fort Calhoun. "Now Mako's on the loose again, and he's got his hooks into this Stanley kid. If I can't find a way to stop it, on October Twenty-Fourth, there's going to be another Operation Aurora. And this one won't be some isolated fake town. It's going worldwide!

You can't believe what happens when everything grinds to a halt!"

Tommy was appalled. "But that's, like, a day and a half away!"

Jax nodded miserably. "And I can't even be sure that Mako's in New York. I just didn't know where else to start. The only thing I knew was I couldn't just sit back and let it happen."

Tommy looked thoughtful. "Well, where was Mako last seen?"

"Stanley's custody hearing," Jax replied readily. "And jail before that. The one place he has a long-term connection to is here in New York — the Sentia Institute uptown. I used to go for training there, remember? But it's closed now."

"What about the building management?" Tommy persisted.

"Building management?"

"My dad's company renovates offices all over the city," Tommy explained. "Every building is run by a company that handles the maintenance and insurance and stuff like that. Who manages Sentia's building?"

Jax had no answer. Yet he felt a faint stirring of hope at the idea that the trail might not have gone completely cold. "I don't know. How can we find out?"

Tommy shrugged. "There has to be a sign somewhere. It's the law."

"You're a lifesaver!" Jax exclaimed. "Can I crash here tonight? I promise to be out of your way first thing in the morning. I'll contact the management company as soon as they open."

"You're doing it again," Tommy accused. "You're closing me out. Of course you'll stay here tonight. And tomorrow, we go to Sentia together."

"This is my problem, not yours," Jax pointed out.

Tommy was insulted. "Your problem *is* my problem — always was, always will be. And if you're right about this Aurora thing, it's everybody's problem. Besides, I have a math test tomorrow, which makes it an excellent day to be someplace else."

For the first time since stepping out of the little cottage in Fort Calhoun, Jax felt that he was no longer alone.

It was after three AM. Jax was padding barefoot down the hall on his way back from the bathroom when he suddenly came face-to-face with Tommy's father.

"'Scuse me," Mr. Cicerelli mumbled, and then stopped dead. "*Jax?* What are you doing here?"

Jax had already decided how he was going to respond if he accidentally bumped into one of Tommy's parents. After his unexplained disappearance, the Cicerellis were going to have a lot of questions, and Jax wasn't prepared to answer any of them. Nothing could be allowed to interfere with his mission here in New York — even if that meant bending the people who had been like second parents to him.

He held Tommy's father with a magnetic gaze until a very bleary PIP image appeared. "You're still asleep," he said quietly. "You didn't see anybody. Go back to bed and get a good night's rest."

In answer, Mr. Cicerelli yawned hugely and the two went their separate ways. As he let himself back into Tommy's room, Jax couldn't help wondering if this would be the last good night's sleep Mr. Cicarelli would enjoy before Elias Mako turned all of humanity inside out.

23

After the Cicerellis both left for work, the boys allowed themselves the luxury of a quick bowl of cereal before setting out on their quest.

"Same old kitchen," Jax observed. "Even the chocolate-milk stain on the ceiling."

"Sorry to bore you," Tommy said sarcastically. "Some of us have been living our regular lives while the army was turning you into their secret weapon."

"I don't want to be a secret weapon. I don't want to be any kind of weapon."

"You were always a weapon, Opus." Tommy countered, blotting at a dribble of milk on his chin. "Even before we knew about this hypnotism thing. You think the girls stared at your googly eyes because of your manliness? And remember that social studies essay? You got a two-week extension and I got a detention for asking!"

Jax grimaced. "I'm nothing compared with the weapon Mako's turning Stanley into."

"Maybe it won't be so bad," Tommy suggested hopefully. "I mean, doing nothing — what's the downside? We used to suffer through a whole year of school so we could get to summer and lie around doing nothing."

Jax tried to explain. "When you're driving a car, and you shut down, the car keeps going. If you're filling your bathtub, the water runs until you flood your apartment, and the one downstairs, too. If you're cooking, the stove stays on, and the fire isn't over until there's nothing left to burn. Now picture that happening all over the city. And the first responders, like police and firemen, they're not moving either. Not that they could get to you if they wanted to — the streets are full of crashed cars and debris from burning buildings. But even the people who aren't in danger will be soon enough, because they can't eat or drink. And the ones who are unaffected by the post-hypnotic suggestion are losing their minds trying to help the ones who are. Need to hear more?"

"Let's go to Sentia," Tommy decided. "I'm getting a stomachache."

In spite of their serious mission, Jax enjoyed the crowded train ride uptown, trading banter with Tommy and inventing creative meanings for the unreadable subway graffiti.

They got off at the Sixty-Eighth Street station, and the feeling of well-being deserted him completely. Everything about this neighborhood said Sentia to Jax. Even Corrado's Pizza, on Lexington and Sixty-Fifth, reminded him of countless lunches with his fellow young hypnos at the institute. It had been in this hole-in-the-wall restaurant where he'd first been approached by Axel Braintree. And just a few blocks south of here was the spot where Axel's life had come to a violent end.

They turned at Corrado's and ventured west on Sixty-Fifth toward Park Avenue. The first sight of the seven-story brownstone, with its winged gryphons and Doric pillars, made Jax's stomach clench involuntarily. Even though Sentia was no longer in existence, the aura of menace hung heavy in the air.

Tommy could sense his tension. "It's just a building, Opus. It can't hurt you."

The dignified brass plaque that identified the institute had been covered with masking tape. A sign had been taped to the inside of the glass doors:

OFFICE SPACE AVAILABLE

THREE FULL FLOORS

CONTACT GALBRAITH PROPERTY MANAGEMENT

There was a telephone number and an address on East Forty-Seventh Street.

"That's not too far away," Tommy urged. "Let's go."

The taxi dropped them off in front of a modern storefront office just in from Second Avenue. The two boys approached the receptionist, who was typing busily at a computer.

"We have some questions about a building you guys manage," Jax informed her.

She looked them up and down, clearly skeptical that two preteens had any business that was worth the attention of Galbraith Property Management. "Can I have the address, please?"

"It's 115 East Sixty-Fifth Street," Jax supplied. "Where the Sentia Institute used to be."

"I'll get the file about which you have inquired." She stood up and disappeared through a door to another part of the office.

"Check to see if there's a forwarding address," Jax called after her. "You know, for mail."

The boys stood, waiting. Five minutes went by. Then ten.

"How long does it take to get one little file?" Jax murmured impatiently.

"Who uses files anymore?" Tommy added. "Why isn't it all on the computer right in front of her?"

Jax snickered. "They must run this place like it's the Stone Age. You heard her — 'I'll get the file about which you have inquired.' Nobody talks like that anymore."

Tommy assumed a very bad British accent. "I cannot find the file, and that is something up with which I shall not put."

Jax's grin faded fast. *About which you have inquired. Up with which I shall not put.* It sounded stilted and funny, like something an eighteenth-century nobleman might say. But hearing it another way, it was strangely robotic —

Like people talk when they're under a post-hypnotic suggestion!

Somebody had bent this woman and implanted a suggestion, probably triggered by the word *Sentia*. It sounded a lot like Mako, lying in wait for anyone who might be trying to track him down.

Jax grabbed Tommy's arm and began hauling him toward the door. "We're leaving."

"But what about the file?"

"It's a trap!"

They started along Forty-Seventh Street, peering anxiously over their shoulders as they ran. About halfway down the block, Jax pulled Tommy into an alley.

"What are you doing?" Tommy demanded. "If this is a trap, the farther away we are, the better!"

"We have to see what happens," Jax told him. "For all we know, Mako's on his way here."

"All the more reason we should be in *Yonkers* by now!" Tommy reasoned.

"Running away isn't going to stop this new Aurora! I have to face him down."

Tommy was horrified. "You can't beat Mako!"

"I couldn't beat him before. I've gotten stronger. I might be able to take him."

"Might?" Tommy repeated. "Can't you do any better than *might*? That guy could make you lie down in front of a bus if you're wrong!"

"Shhh!" Jax hissed. "Check out that cab."

A yellow taxi drove along Forty-Seventh Street, slowing to a near halt in front of Galbraith Property Management.

"Is it Mako?" Tommy whispered.

"I can't see. The driver's in the way." Gripping the bricks, Jax leaned a little farther out of the alley.

His appearance was greeted by a pointing finger from the backseat of the cab, an urgent command from the passenger. The taxi peeled away from the curb.

"Follow me!" Jax barked.

The instruction was unnecessary. The two boys barreled down the alley, threading their way through trash cans and stacks of boxes. A roar from behind drew Jax's attention over his shoulder. The cab was in the narrow passage, coming after them, swerving around obstacles. The front bumper smacked into a blue recycling box, showering them with a blizzard of shredded paper.

"Either there's a ticker-tape parade or he's right behind us!" Tommy wailed, knees pumping.

They blasted out onto Forty-Sixth Street scant seconds ahead of their pursuer, and scrambled along the sidewalk, trying to lose themselves in the pedestrians. The taxi jounced out of the alley and wheeled to follow them. Jax and Tommy ran flat out, rounding the corner onto First Avenue. But the cab was too fast, making the turn onto the wide thoroughfare and pulling even with them.

It's no use! Jax thought desperately. *We'll never outrun a car!*

There was a sudden squeal of brakes, and the taxi disappeared from his peripheral vision. He held up an instant to glance over his shoulder, and Tommy plowed into him from behind, nearly bowling him over.

"What are you doing, man? Keep going!"

"Look!" rasped Jax.

The taxi was now hopelessly trapped in the traffic jam caused by a series of barriers and lane closures. Across the street towered the glass front of the United Nations building, surrounded by its fountains and fluttering flags.

"Let's get out of here before the avenue starts moving again!" Tommy urged.

Jax led his friend into the entryway of a parking garage. "Listen — now that they've lost me, I'm going to double back and take the taxi by surprise."

"What part of scramming don't you understand?" Tommy exploded.

"When the cab was chasing me, I had to escape," Jax explained. "But now I have the upper hand, since they won't expect me to come back. I'll sneak up and climb in, hypnotizing on the move. Even if it's Mako, I think I can get it done."

"I'll go with you," Tommy decided.

Jax shook his head. "You'll be defenseless."

Tommy reached down and picked up an empty champagne bottle. "Not quite."

They doubled back via the garage's circular drive, reemerging onto First Avenue a short distance behind the stopped cab. The traffic jam was getting worse, with horns honking and drivers announcing their irritation in colorful language.

Crouching low, they stepped amid the stopped vehicles and crept up on the taxi. Jax scanned the rear window for Mako's three-hundred-dollar haircut, but the sun was reflecting off the glass, and he couldn't get a good look.

Wordlessly, Jax directed their approach, himself on the left, Tommy on the right. He mouthed the words: *On three.*

One, two . . .

Jax flung the cab door wide and jumped in, blazing with all the mesmeric power he could muster. Tommy burst in the other side, bottle raised, ready to strike.

"No!" Jax reached out and grabbed his friend's wrist a split second before the magnum smashed down on the passenger's head.

24

A petite, brown-haired girl Jax's age looked up at them with frightened eyes. "Jax?"

"This isn't Mako!" Tommy blurted.

"It's Kira Kendall!" Jax breathed. "We were hypnos together at Sentia!"

"If you're not going anywhere, get out of my cab," the driver tossed over his shoulder. "Especially you with the bottle."

Kira gave the man a ten-dollar bill, and the three exited the taxi, coming to stand in the shadow of the UN building.

"Are you spying for Mako?" Jax demanded harshly.

Her face crumpled. "I'm so sorry, Jax! You were right, and I was wrong! He's horrible! A monster! And who knows what awful things he has planned!"

"*I* do," Jax said bitterly. "I can't even begin to describe it. He has to be stopped."

She nodded vigorously. "I've been trying to trap him for the police! That's why I bent the receptionist at Galbraith. I gave her a suggestion to text me if anybody asked about Sentia. I took off out of French class thinking I'd be chasing Dr. Mako!"

"The police can't hold Mako," Jax told her. "A maximum-security prison didn't hold him. And now he's found another kid who can hypnotize by video." The whole story poured out — Fort Calhoun and HoWaRD, the devastation in Delta Prime, Stanley and this new Aurora-like plan that would do unimaginable damage worldwide.

Kira listened, her eyes widening in shock. Even Tommy, who already knew, was gray in the face listening to the appalling details.

"If what you say is true, the post-hypnotic suggestion is already out there," said Kira in a hopeless tone. "For all we know, it's in *us*. I go on FreeForAll. Don't you?"

Jax nodded grimly. "Which means tomorrow at nine AM, we'll probably grind to a halt along with everybody else."

"Nine AM?" Kira repeated. "That's exactly when the big UN conference is supposed to start!"

Jax was instantly alert. "UN conference?"

Tommy indicated the traffic snarl on First Avenue. "That's why all these lanes are blocked off. They've stepped up security because the big muck-a-mucks are already starting to arrive. It's the first time in history that every leader of every country is going to be under the same roof. The TV news can't shut up about it." He made a face. "It's going to be a pretty big bust if the whole world stops on a dime the minute it's supposed to start."

Light dawned on Jax. "Don't you see? That's classic Mako! It can't be a coincidence that he scheduled his Aurora for exactly that instant."

Kira nodded breathlessly. "They're expecting the largest TV, Internet, and media audience of all time for the opening ceremony. He's going to unleash this monster at the very moment when the eyes of the planet are focused on a single spot."

"But what can we do about it?" asked Tommy. "We're just kids."

"The only person who can stop this is the one who started it — Mako himself," Jax said with conviction. "I've never been able to bend him before, but I have to try again."

Tommy hefted his champagne bottle. "And if you're having trouble, I can help."

"That's the last thing you can do," Kira pointed out. "Even if we knock him unconscious and tie him to a chair to keep him away from the UN, that won't stop the Aurora. Our only hope is to hypnotize him into calling it off before it happens."

Tommy looked worried. "*Can* he call it off?"

"He can," Jax confirmed. "He just needs Stanley to record a new video for FreeForAll. It may not reach every single person, but it should minimize the damage. At least the whole world won't stand still."

"But you can do that yourself," Kira reasoned. "You hypnotized remotely before this kid Stanley ever did."

Jax shook his head. "Even if I made a video, it would never reach enough people to make a difference. Mako must have hackers who can get his message on FreeForAll. Kira, when you bent that receptionist at Galbraith, did you happen to notice if there's a forwarding address for the Sentia Institute?"

She did not look encouraged. "It's just a post-office box. Somewhere in New Jersey." She reached into her pocket and produced a crumpled slip of paper. "Pine Bough, New Jersey. Box one-seventeen."

"It's in the burbs somewhere, not too far away," Tommy put in.

"It's a place to start," Jax decided. "And it's our only lead."

Kira took out her phone and began tapping at it, accessing commuter schedules. "The next bus to Pine Bough isn't until two thirty, from the Port Authority. I'll drop my school stuff at home and meet you at the gate." All at once, her face drained of color. "Uh-oh . . ."

"What is it?" Jax asked in concern.

In answer, she turned the screen to them. Beside the charts of destinations, departures, and arrivals was a flashing notice, captioned *Runaway*.

INTERSTATE ALERT
IF YOU SEE THIS BOY
CONTACT POLICE IMMEDIATELY

There was a photograph of a sandy-haired youth with large luminous eyes.

It was Jackson Opus.

25

Jax adjusted his Mets cap and, in his heart, asked his beloved Yankees to forgive him. The sunglasses, which had cost five dollars from a street vendor, were heavy and seemed determined to slide off his nose.

"Keep your shades on," Tommy advised in an anxious undertone. "You made the news."

Inside the terminal, a video screen provided stock market quotes, a crawl of headlines, and TV news stories. There was Jax's picture over the caption *Missing Boy.*

As they bought their tickets, the woman at the kiosk wouldn't stop staring at Jax. He flipped up his glasses and stared back. "I am six-foot-seven, and Chinese."

"Have a nice trip," she said, passing their change through the slot.

"Good one," Tommy approved. "When you see Kira, tell her that I've got big muscles, and I look like the guy from *Twilight.* She just texted. She's here already, waiting for us at the gate."

Kira was pacing nervously in the waiting area. "I was afraid you got arrested," she whispered to Jax.

"The ticket lady got too curious, but I took care of it. And by the way, Tommy looks like the guy from *Twilight.*"

"Not the creepy one," Tommy put in.

"There was a cop here before," she went on, "walking past the gate and peering into faces. He's gone now, but who knows for how long?"

Jax consulted his watch. "We're supposed to leave in ten minutes. Why aren't they letting us on?"

The bus was parked six feet short of the loading marker. The door was shut and, through the glass, they could see the driver savoring every bite of his Big Mac.

Tommy squeezed Jax's arm. "Dude —"

It was the police officer, strolling through the gathering crowd in the direction of Gate 62.

Kira knocked on the door of the bus. "Can we come aboard now?"

The driver never glanced away from his burger. One of the other commuters laughed. "I guess you're new to this bus. Vlado wouldn't put down his sandwich if the terminal was on fire."

Kira knocked again. "Hey, mister! I sprained my ankle, and I really need to sit down!"

The driver licked a sesame seed off his mustache and paid her no mind.

The cop passed Gate 60, and kept coming.

Tommy sidled up to Jax. "Should we run?"

Jax shook his head. "That'll just tip him off that something's fishy. Besides, we need to make this bus. Every hour is precious."

The officer was only twenty feet away now, strolling through the crowd, obviously on alert. His eyes panned the line of waiting passengers.

Is he looking at me?

Jax's hand rose to the temple of his sunglasses. He would bend this cop if he had to, but that carried a new risk. He would be unmasking himself in front of all these people. Surely some of them had seen his picture on TV. One of the first things he'd learned about hypnotism was that no one was powerful enough to bend everybody.

Ten feet. The officer was heading straight for him. He had to act —

At that moment, Vlado finished his sandwich, pulled the bus up to the loading point, and opened the door. Holding his breath, Jax turned his back on the cop, lined up with the others, and filed aboard. With every step, he expected to feel an iron grip on his shoulder. It never came. The officer moved on with a little wave in Vlado's direction, and continued to Gate 63.

Jax handed over his ticket and collapsed in his seat. In the opposite row, he could see Kira, her face pinched.

Tommy took the place between them. "Man, if it's this hard just to get on the bus . . ."

He never finished the sentence, but his message was obvious:

How would they muster the strength for what lay ahead?

Although Pine Bough, New Jersey, was located less than twenty miles from the Lincoln Tunnel, it seemed like another universe. Nestled in rolling hills, it was a picture-book town of picket fences, charming wood-frame homes, and mature shade trees.

"Look at this place," said Tommy in awe. "It looks like a movie set for Anytown, USA."

Jax, whose father had once managed a Bentley dealership in New York, instantly recognized the many luxury automobiles parked on Main Street. "Not Anytown," he amended. "Moneytown. This is for wealthy people who want to be close to New York, but also want to feel like they're out in the country."

Tommy considered this. "Well, Mako's rich, right? At least, he can always get money by bending people into giving it to him."

"Sentia's mail is forwarded to a PO box in this town." Kira pointed up the road. "There's the post office. Let's go in there and see what we can find out."

The United States Post Office, Pine Bough Station, was a tiny facility with a single clerk who had more work than she could seem to handle. She answered the phone, weighed packages, sold stamps, and prepared passport applications for a long line of customers.

Jax, Tommy, and Kira snaked their way through the standees to the wall of mailboxes. Jax felt a tingle of fear and anticipation. This was his first connection with Dr. Mako since the horrible day Axel had died.

There it was — box number 117. It was identical to all the others, a narrow square metal front with a slot for a key none of them had.

Tommy was the first to put their disappointment into words. "That's it? We just stand here and look at it?"

"We're just hypnotists," Jax shot back. "We don't have X-ray vision."

159

"We can bend the clerk into opening it up for us," Kira decided, "but we can't just push in front of all these people. The best we can do is get in line and wait our turn."

They took their place at the back of the queue, inching forward at a snail's pace.

Jax glanced over at the mailbox. "Mako's box," he murmured aloud. "He comes in here, takes out a key, gets his mail."

"Or maybe not," Tommy mused. "Maybe when Sentia closed up, he had to give an address, so he wrote down any old thing. And that box belongs to some little old lady who can't figure out why she keeps getting Sentia's electric bill."

"It's our only lead," Jax decided. "Mako's mail is a connection to Mako."

Kira looked sad. "I still can't believe what Dr. Mako has turned into. He taught me so much. I thought he was a great man."

"I was just as fooled as you," Jax soothed her. "Then he tried to kill my parents. And me. And he did kill Axel Braintree."

"I was so stupid!" she lamented. "Even if I couldn't see it in Mako, I should have known about Wilson. I thought he was just a bully who liked to throw his weight around."

"Mako uses people," said Jax bitterly. "Wilson was his muscle, we were his research, and Stanley's his" — what had Brassmeyer called it? — "his doomsday machine. Stanley's message is, anyway."

"Have you still got that on tape?" Tommy asked.

Jax took out his phone, beckoned his friends close, and replayed the recording he had made of Stanley's clip on FreeForAll.

"You will stay perfectly still until you hear this special word — the name of what I'm holding in my hand right now. Remember it well. . . ."

"And what was it?" Tommy prompted.

"I didn't dare look," Jax replied. "The kid can bend me. If I'd watched it, I'd risk going under. Then I wouldn't even have this much information."

Kira leaned in closer to the phone. "Play it again."

As the recording restarted, her brow furrowed. "Do you hear that in the background? Horses."

Jax listened closely. She was right. There was definitely some kind of animal — more than one. "How can you be sure it's horses?"

"I used to be big into horseback riding," she explained. "I had to give it up when Dr. Mako recruited me for Sentia, but I was really good. When this message was recorded, there were horses in the background. I recognize the whinnying, and you can even hear the clopping of hoofs." She looked up in excitement. "Horses. Definitely."

"Central Park?" Tommy suggested.

She shook her head. "Then you'd hear city noises, too. This is more like a horse farm, or riding stable." She turned to a well-dressed woman ahead of them in line. "Excuse me, are there any horse farms around here?"

The woman laughed. "Only about thirty."

"Thirty," Jax repeated faintly. It was like taking one step forward, then two steps back. Just when it seemed like they'd made a breakthrough, the task ahead of them became even more daunting than before. How could three kids, on foot, investigate thirty horse farms by tomorrow at nine AM?

"This is horse country," the woman explained. "The United States Olympic team boards their mounts here. We have stud farms and racing stables. A lot of people keep horses on their properties. Why, there's a huge spread just south of town belonging to that billionaire who died a few months ago — Avery Quackenbush."

Quackenbush! Jax felt a rush of total understanding. Avery Quackenbush had been under Mako's influence. It all made sense!

"That's the one!" Jax whispered excitedly when the woman had turned away from them.

Tommy was bewildered. "How do you figure that?"

"Mako had his hooks into Quackenbush. Now that the billionaire's dead, he's using the property as a hideout and headquarters! That's where Stanley recorded the message for FreeForAll."

"We have to get out there," Kira decided. "Do they have taxis here?"

"Too suspicious," said Jax. "This is a small town where everybody knows everybody else. Three kids — outsiders — can't just stand in the middle of town, waving at cabs. Not when my face is all over TV and the Internet."

"What are we supposed to do?" Tommy challenged. "Walk?"

"Yes."

"It could be miles," Kira protested. "It's already after four o'clock. We'll never find the place once it gets dark."

"We start off walking," Jax clarified, "and when we're out of town a little, we flag down a car and bend the driver."

They began to push through the crowded post office toward the door. Jax was aware of a heightened buzz of conversation behind them. But he paid no attention until something squeezed his wrist. He wheeled to face the postal clerk. She grasped his arm with one hand; in the other, she clutched a printout that was all too familiar.

The *Missing Boy* poster.

26

He flipped up his glasses to bend her, but she would not meet his eyes. Why couldn't he reach her? All at once, he had the answer: He couldn't hypnotize her because she was already hypnotized — by Kira.

"Let go," Kira said in a low but forceful tone.

The clerk complied, and they made for the exit.

A broad-shouldered man blocked their way. "What's going on here?"

Before Jax could respond hypnotically, Tommy stomped on the man's foot. The man hopped aside with a yelp, and the three New Yorkers slipped outside. No one was thinking about the Quackenbush horse farm now. All that mattered was getting away from the post office.

A squad car screeched up to the curb, and a uniformed officer leaped out. With a sinking heart, Jax realized that the postal clerk must have alerted the police before coming after him. He toyed with the idea of making eye contact with the cop, but quickly abandoned it. It was hard to bend a moving target at a distance. The only solution was to get moving himself.

"Run!" he bellowed, then followed his own advice,

tearing off down the street. Tommy and Kira were hot on his heels.

The officer was an athlete, and matched them stride for stride, closing the gap. Jax hurdled a low hedge and pounded into the town square, plowing through a bed of chrysanthemums. Desperately, he scanned the area, looking for any possible means of escape. Pine Bough was a tiny town, so there was plenty of running room. But how would they ever lose the cop who was chasing them?

The letup in his concentration cost him dearly. With a crunching of tires on gravel, a second squad car jumped the curb and pulled directly into his path. It was too late for Jax to adjust his course. All he could do was hold out his arms to soften the impact. He bounced off the side of the car and hit the ground hard. As he rolled across the grass, he knocked the feet out from under his pursuer. The man went down like a sack of oats and lay on top of Jax, stunned.

The driver of the second cruiser was an older man, portly and slow moving. He reached for Tommy, who nimbly sidestepped him and sprinted away.

Kira tried a different approach. She locked eyes with the older cop, hoping to bend him quickly. But something blocked her, something she could not penetrate.

Though slow, the older cop was as strong as an ox. The instant he clamped on to her arm, she knew she was caught.

Jax tried to scramble back up, but the younger officer put a hammerlock on him.

"Cool your jets, kid! You're not going anywhere!"

Utterly defeated, he spotted Kira, also in custody. And Tommy?

"Where's the other kid?" the older cop wheezed.

Jax inclined his head, scanning the area. There was no sign of Tommy. He allowed himself the slightest glimmer of hope. As long as they had an ally on the loose, all was not completely lost.

Tommy ran flat out — up streets, around corners, and through backyards. He had not spared the time to see his companions captured, but he knew they had been. Things looked bad for them — or maybe not. Jax could get anybody to do anything.

Tommy had once been jealous of that ability; now he was counting on it. And Kira was a hypnotist, too. He would never understand their power, but he'd seen too much not to appreciate what they were capable of. They might be able to mesmerize themselves free again. That meant he had to stay free, too, to meet up with them when they got away. He had to believe it still wasn't too late to stop Mako.

Tommy had no paranormal power. For him, the key to staying free was hiding. But where? Where could he lie low in a place where any stranger stood out like a sore thumb?

That was when he spied the construction site. An old house was in the process of being knocked down, probably to be replaced with some McMansion. Work seemed to be complete for the day — at least, the site was quiet. That made this the perfect place to chill out until Jax and Kira made their next move.

Slowing only a little, he placed two hands on top of the safety fence and vaulted up and over. He was already in midair when he saw the Bobcat mini-digger parked just inside the perimeter. It was too late to change direction. Gravity didn't work that way. His head slammed against the raised metal shovel attachment. The impact was even more devastating than he expected it to be. His last thought before everything went dark was *Why do I let Jackson Opus get me into these things?*

Then he crumpled to the ground, and remembered no more.

27

In his office in the HoWaRD building at Fort Calhoun, Captain Pedroia was shutting down his computer for the day when the door was flung wide, and in burst none other than Colonel Brassmeyer.

Pedroia stood up. "Colonel?" This was highly unusual. If the commander wanted to see someone, he'd send his aide. It was rare for him to show up in person.

"The plane's waiting for us on the tarmac, wheels up in fifteen minutes."

"Where are we going?"

"Jackson Opus is in custody in Pine Bough, New Jersey, just west of New York," Brassmeyer told him.

"New Jersey?" the psychiatrist repeated. "Surely we've got soldiers in the area who can scoop him up and bring him here."

Brassmeyer smiled without humor. "I'd rather crawl there on broken glass than have to explain to anybody why they don't dare look that kid in the eye."

Pedroia swallowed hard. "I'll get my jacket."

The police station in Pine Bough was a little corner of the town hall on a short cul-de-sac off the main square.

It had two desks, a locker room, and a single holding cell. Even the bathroom was shared with the Sanitation Department office across the hall.

Jax and Kira paced anxiously as the precious minutes before tomorrow at nine AM ticked away. They were watched over by the older cop, who turned out to be the local police chief. It should have been easy — one jailor, two hypnotists. He should have been bent, and they should have been gone by now.

But it wasn't happening. Time and time again, one or the other would call the man over to ask an "important question," and fix him with a practiced mesmeric stare. They would look at him, he would look back at them, but the hypnotic link — and the familiar PIP image — would not even begin to form. It was as baffling as it was frustrating — until the old officer called home to inform his wife that he'd be detained at work indefinitely to look after two "runaways." The conversation soon turned to the old man's upcoming cataract surgery, and Jax and Kira had their answer.

"Cataracts!" Kira lamented. "They must cloud his vision just enough to protect him from being bent."

"Tommy's still out there," Jax whispered. "He's our only hope."

"He can't stop Mako on his own," Kira scoffed. "It's a long shot for the two of us. He isn't even a hypno."

Jax bit his lip. He couldn't picture Tommy going after Mako, but he also couldn't see him giving up. There was a core of loyalty to Tommy's character that would prevent him from getting on a bus back to New York and writing

Jax and Kira off. It was no match for hypnotic ability, but it was a kind of mule-headedness that you could never count out.

On the other hand, the kid wasn't Superman. Just because he was persistent didn't mean he could defeat cops and rip open steel bars.

Come on, Tommy! Where are you?

The distant crowing of a rooster was confusing. They crowed in the morning, but it was dark. Pitch black, in fact. Then Tommy felt the vibrating in his pocket. His phone! The new ring tone, freshly downloaded, was the cock-a-doodle-doo of a rooster.

In order to reach into his pocket, he had to sit up. And that was definitely a bad idea. His head all but exploded. The word *pain* didn't even begin to describe it.

It came back to him then, in reverse order: the crack of his skull striking the Bobcat's shovel, his flight from the police, the capture of his companions. His memory took him all the way back to the moment last night when Jax had come in his window and told him about the terrible plan Dr. Mako was about to unleash on the world.

Dr. Mako, who was right here in Pine Bough, on a horse farm south of town —

The rooster was still crowing. But by the time he managed to pull out his phone, the sound had stopped. Good thing he hadn't answered it. It was his parents, probably frantic by now because he hadn't come home from school. They were going to kill him.

He thumbed a quick text in reply: *Sorry to worry u. Forgot to call. Sleeping over at Ralph's tonight.* There was no such person as Ralph, and Mom and Dad probably knew it. But at least hearing from him was proof that he wasn't, as Mom always put it, "dead in a ditch somewhere."

He knew the message had reached Mom and Dad because, a few seconds after he sent it, the rooster started crowing again, and the word *home* appeared on the screen. This wasn't fun for a guy with a really nasty headache. He had no intention of answering. With so much at stake, he couldn't imagine a conversation with his parents doing anything but complicating an already messy situation.

An odd thought came to him. The very first time he'd been hypnotized, at a stage show, he'd been commanded to crow like a rooster. Could he be hypnotized now? Was that why everything seemed so weird? He raised his hand to his aching head. Blood. Hypnotism couldn't make you bleed.

Speaking of hypnotism, why hadn't Jax and Kira called? Surely they had bent their way out of custody by now. He checked the clock on his phone, and did a double take.

It was *ten thirty*! He'd been out for hours!

He brought up the call log. Nothing from the others. Could they still be in jail? Why? Something must have gone very wrong.

He stood, which brought on a head rush that very nearly knocked him over. Only his innate stubbornness kept him on his feet. When the world stabilized, he went back to his phone, and Googled *Where is police station, Pine Bough, NJ?*

An address appeared. He remembered the street name coming off the main square — Law Lane. He would find it. He *had* to find it.

He eased himself over the fence and started off through the darkened neighborhood. His head still throbbed abominably, but he felt more steady and alert with every step. There were a few lights on in houses, but the streets were deserted. Tommy was used to New York, where there were people out at any hour of the day or night. Here in Pine Bough, they rolled up the sidewalks after dinner.

There it was — Law Lane. Even if he'd missed the street sign, he would have seen the squad car parked outside. He approached cautiously, reflecting that he had already escaped the Pine Bough P.D. And now here he was, walking straight into their police station. What if Jax and Kira were already off battling Mako, and he was delivering himself on a silver platter?

There was only one way to find out.

The placard read:

PINE BOUGH MUNICIPAL CENTER
POLICE STATION
LAW COURT

He pushed open the door and stepped inside.

The office was small and drab, with two desks head to head and, at the back, a holding cell with floor-to-ceiling steel bars. There, the picture of dejection, sat —

"Jax! Kira!" Tommy hissed.

Jax jumped up so suddenly that the chair he'd been sitting on overturned. "Tommy, what happened to you? You're all beat up!"

"I bumped my head," Tommy croaked. "Don't worry. It hurts worse than it looks. But never mind that — where are the cops?"

"There's only one — the older guy," Kira explained briskly. "He went out to get us some food. Quick — find the keys and let us out of here!"

"Right!" Egged on by the prisoners, Tommy began to ransack the two desks. No key.

"Over there!" Jax pointed to a wall hook where a small key dangled.

Tommy raced over and grabbed it, then jammed it into the lock in the cell door. It wouldn't turn.

"Keep looking!" Jax urged. "Hurry! He could be back any minute!"

Frantically, Tommy circled the room, scanning every wall and bulletin board. He even tried the Sanitation office across the hall, but none of their keys fit the cell. He was about to try the courtroom, when a voice announced, "I was able to scrounge up a couple of turkey sandwiches. Hope that'll hold you —"

And then the police chief was frozen in the doorway, a

white paper bag in his hand. His eyes fell on Tommy, who was in the process of rifling through a uniform jacket that was hanging from a coat tree.

"All right, son, no worries," he said, almost kindly. "They can make another sandwich for you."

In answer, Tommy made a bull run at the police chief. Dropping the white bag, the man reached for him. Tommy knew only this: *Everything* depended on him getting past the cop at the door. At the last second, he ducked low and squeezed out under the man's elbow. The instant he felt the cool air of the night, he was up to a full sprint and gone, disappearing into the darkness.

The chief considered giving chase for about three seconds, then heaved a resigned sigh. "I don't suppose either of you would like to tell me your friend's name so I can get in touch with his parents." There was no reply. "Looks like he tore his face up pretty good. Maybe he needs a doctor." Still nothing.

"Fine." He gave them their dinner, sat down at his desk, and picked up the phone. "I hate to bother you, Wisnewski, but the third kid just paid us a visit here. I tried to grab him, but he gave me the slip. Do you mind having a look around for him? I'd love to turn all three of them over when the army gets here."

Inside the cell, Jax looked up in alarm. *The army?*

"Yeah, you heard me," the chief went on into the phone. "The kid from the poster turns out to be some kind of military brat who took off. Not sure how the other two fit in, but they'll be out of our hair tonight.

Can't be too soon for me. I like things nice and sleepy around here."

Jax, who was starving, suddenly couldn't take so much as a single bite of his sandwich. The army was coming to get him. He should have known. Who else could have circulated those alerts? And when the Pine Bough P.D. had reported they had the runaway in question, the information had been passed along the law enforcement network until it reached Fort Calhoun and Colonel Brassmeyer.

Kira regarded him questioningly, but he could offer no more than a hopeless shrug. On top of all his other regrets — and there were many — how could he have been crazy enough to involve Tommy and Kira in this mess? He felt horrible about it but, in the end, he supposed it wouldn't make much difference. Nine o'clock tomorrow morning would still roll around, and nothing would ever be the same again.

So wrapped up was he in his misery that at first he failed to notice the distant roar of an unmuffled engine. Soon, though, the noise grew louder, until it was impossible to ignore it.

"What *is* that?" Kira whispered.

Jax could only shake his head. It reminded him a little of the tanks on maneuvers outside Fort Calhoun. And for an insane moment, he actually toyed with the possibility that Brassmeyer was so mad at him, he had driven an M1 all the way from Oklahoma just for the pleasure of blowing Jax's head off.

The police chief was on his feet now, frowning in confusion as he pondered what in Pine Bough made so much noise, especially in the middle of the night. The floor was vibrating now, and the glass windowpanes, too.

And then the front door of the police station disintegrated into a shower of flying splinters, along with the doorframe and eight inches of plaster wall on either side.

28

Out of the blizzard of dust and debris roared the Bobcat, Tommy Cicerelli at the controls.

Jax and Kira ran to the front of their cell, staring in openmouthed wonder.

"Get back!" Tommy bellowed. He adjusted the digger to the level of the lock and wrenched the controls. The Bobcat surged ahead, its heavy metal scoop smashing into the lock, bending steel bars and knocking the cell door askew.

The police chief raced forward, but the cell door came down on him, pinning him to the floor. He struggled, but the weight of the digger kept the bars in place.

Tommy cut the engine and jumped down to the rubble-strewn floor. "Sorry," he tossed in the direction of the police chief. He reached in through the opening and hauled Jax and Kira out of the cell.

Flattened to the floor, the chief was beside himself. "What are you kids?"

"We're not bad," Jax tried to explain. "We're just in a hurry. A really big hurry. We'll send help — you know, later."

They ran off into the night, heading in the direction they hoped was south.

"That was awesome, Tommy!" Jax panted. "Where'd you learn to drive a Bobcat?"

"My dad is in construction, remember? I've been doing it since I was eight."

"How are we going to find that horse farm in the dark?" Kira wondered. "It could be miles from here."

At that moment, there was the blurp of a siren, and a spotlight shone on them, three insects trapped in amber. "Freeze!" came a voice through the loudspeaker. It was the other cop, Wisnewski.

"Back off," said Jax quietly. "I've got this."

Wisnewski got out of his car and approached, hand-cuffs at the ready. "All right, you lot. Into the car."

Jax turned to face him, moving closer because of the darkness. "You're very calm . . . very relaxed." The PIP image appeared — himself in the cruiser's spotlight, Tommy and Kira a safe distance behind him. "It's your urgent desire to take us down to the old Quackenbush farm. . . . Nothing in the world could make you happier."

Within minutes, they were in the squad car, heading south.

"Excellent," Jax approved. "Every mile makes you that much more content. Now, after you drop us off, you'll forget all about us and where we are. . . . Oh, yeah, and you'll go back to the police station and get your boss out from under the cell door."

"These'll help," added Tommy, reaching from the backseat to drop the keys to the Bobcat into the cup holder.

After about ten minutes, the squad car veered off the highway. The high beams illuminated a tall archway bearing only the letter Q.

"Kill the lights," Jax ordered. "We want to — uh — surprise them."

They continued about a quarter mile on the gravel drive. In the gloom, Jax could make out fenced pastureland on either side.

Kira pointed. "Look."

Up ahead they could see the main house, huge and rambling. Sure enough, there were lights on.

Jax's stomach tightened as he contemplated the fact that Mako might be inside, and that their confrontation was near.

"Okay," he told Wisnewski, "stop right here."

The officer waited only long enough for them to get out of the car before turning around and speeding away toward town to complete his hypnotic instructions.

As they made their stealthy approach to the house, Tommy's phone went off with its symphony of cock-a-doodle-doo.

"Shhh!" Jax and Kira chorused.

Sheepishly, Tommy silenced it. "My folks. They've been calling all night."

"I bent my parents before meeting you guys at the bus station," Kira put in. "I hate to do that, but I had the feeling that this was going to turn into a long day."

"Must be nice," Tommy grumbled. "I'm going to end up grounded till I'm forty."

"The whole world's going to end up grounded if we can't pull this off," Jax reminded them.

The house was nowhere near as big as the vast Quackenbush estate Jax had visited in Connecticut, but it was still an impressive home, with several wings stretching out in all directions.

They ducked into the bushes and began to trace the perimeter, peering into windows as they moved along. Most of the rooms were empty, but there was a dim glow attesting to the fact that lights were on elsewhere.

They moved to another window, and there he was — Stanley X, lying on the couch with his bare feet on an ottoman, watching TV. He seemed so young, so ordinary, so harmless that it was hard to imagine that he was Mako's instrument in the coming global disaster. He was a little kid, an eight-year-old in Angry Birds pajamas, up past his bedtime watching cartoons.

Tommy peered over Jax's shoulder. "That's Stanley? Him? He looks like a Cub Scout!"

"He definitely doesn't seem like the architect of the end of the world," Kira agreed.

"The army thinks he's the only known Arcanov," Jax told them, "and his power is second to none. In the hands of a guy like Mako, he could be the most dangerous person alive."

The most dangerous person alive giggled at something on the screen.

"Where's Mako?" Tommy asked.

"Probably not far away," Jax concluded. "He's Stanley's legal guardian now. And anyway, you can't leave an eight-year-old all alone in the middle of nowhere."

"So what's our plan?" Kira probed.

"This could be our only shot at Stanley without Mako around," Jax decided. "I'm going to go in there and talk to him. Maybe I can convince him that Mako's evil and he should join up with us."

"And if you can't?" she persisted.

"Then I'll try to bend him."

"You said he bends *you*!" Tommy protested.

Jax glared at him. "What are you — my nanny? I have to try. This isn't optional, and it can't wait. It's now or never!"

They moved on to the next window, which opened on a deserted hallway. One by one, they climbed over the sill and closed the sash silently behind them. Jax in the lead, they tiptoed down the corridor to the parlor where Stanley was watching TV.

Jax stepped inside. "Hi, Stanley."

Surprised, the boy sat bolt upright. "Jax — what are you doing here?"

Jax advanced slowly, cautiously. He didn't want to upset the eight-year-old, but he had to tell the truth. It was after midnight, which made this the day of the UN conference.

He couldn't waste time. There wasn't any left.

"I've got to tell you some stuff, Stanley, and it may not be so easy for you to hear." He moved closer, doing his best to be unthreatening. "Ferguson — Mako — whatever he told you his name is — he isn't your relative. He's a bad guy — a *really* bad guy, and he's using your power to do something terrible."

Stanley's eyes flashed with anger. "It's not true!"

Jax felt a twinge of hypnotic stirring, and adjusted his gaze slightly off-center. If Stanley could pack that much mesmeric punch in a resentful glance, the kid was even more dangerous than Jax had suspected.

"It *is* true," Jax persisted. "I'm sorry to have to tell you. Remember that video clip he made you record —?"

And then an overpowering force grabbed Jax from behind, locking him in a chokehold. A knee in the small of his back lifted his heels slightly off the floor. He tried to rasp "Mako!" but no sound would come out. He hung there, paralyzed with pain.

"Hello, Dopus!" came an all-too-familiar sneer.

29

Not Mako. *Wilson*.

"You're at Fort Calhoun!" Jax gasped.

"I guess geography isn't your jam," Wilson replied with a cruel laugh. "I was never under army protection like you. I could quit anytime I wanted. Good move on my part. I've been itching to get my hands on you for a long time."

Suddenly, Wilson pitched forward, releasing his grip on Jax.

Jax wheeled to see Tommy clinging to Wilson's back, his hands clutched around the big teenager's throat. Wilson spun around in an attempt to dislodge his attacker. Tommy held on for dear life. A swinging sneaker knocked a lamp off an end table. It hit the floor and shattered.

Stanley stood up on the sofa, his distress evident. "Stop it!"

Jax tried to lock eyes with Wilson, but the older boy was moving too much in his battle with Tommy. Jax charged his enemy, grabbed him around the midsection, and drove forward like a wrestler. Wilson staggered back a few steps into the TV stand. All three combatants *and* the

TV hit the floor. The screen cracked but, amazingly, the cartoons continued.

Tommy, crushed by Wilson, emitted an *"Oof!"* that almost drowned out Stanley's wailing.

Jax pressed his advantage, crawling on top of Wilson and forcing his eyes into his adversary's line of vision. With a roar of protest, Wilson swatted him away with a backhand like the kick of a mule. Tommy reached around and managed to press the heel of his hand into Wilson's nose. With a cry of outrage, the burly teen brought his elbow into Tommy's ribs.

With a winded whimper, Tommy let go, and Wilson leaped up and made a run at Jax, slamming him into the doorframe. Jax blinked away the stars that were consuming his vision and tried once more to press his sole advantage with this huge opponent — to focus his hypnotic gaze on Wilson.

"Don't even think about it, Dopus!" he raged, averting his eyes. "All I have to do is turn my face three inches away! I can still see well enough to pound you into hamburger!"

And then another voice — a female one — said, "Wilson."

Kira appeared in the doorway, moving into Wilson's line of sight. Before he could react, she had him. "You are very calm . . . very relaxed. . . ."

Fighting to avoid being bent, Wilson turned, only to be caught by Jax's eyes, which were darkening through blue into purple. "Easy, Wilson," he told his enemy. "Chill out. . . . No reason to get excited. . . ."

Stanley made a move to wade into the fray, but Tommy blocked him.

Jax could sense that Wilson was nearly his. "You're feeling great, big guy . . . just go with it." When the PIP image appeared, Jax could see a gigantic welt on his left cheek where Wilson had smashed him. "We're all friends here. . . ."

"Sure," Tommy muttered. "What's a few broken ribs between friends?"

Kira shot him a harsh "Shhh!"

"Okay," Jax went on when he sensed that the connection was solid. "Now you're going to take us to Dr. Mako. Don't make a fuss; don't say anything. Just lead us quietly to the room he's in."

Wilson just stood there, his expression haunted.

"Come on now, it's just a walk down the hall. . . . Think how wonderful it'll feel to stretch your legs. . . ."

"Maybe you didn't bend him right?" Tommy suggested.

"That's not it," Kira put in. "Mako must have programmed him not to answer certain questions."

"All right, Wilson," Jax persisted, "any suggestion in your mind that was planted by Dr. Mako is not important anymore. . . . All that matters is what great friends we've turned into, and how we're both on the same side. Dr. Mako needs to know about that, so please take me to him. . . ."

Wilson began to whimper.

"You have to back off," Kira counseled. "He's carrying

conflicting commands from you and Mako. If you push it, you could damage his mind."

"Like he's got a mind to damage," scoffed Tommy.

"You guys have got it all wrong!" Stanley piped up. "He couldn't obey if he wanted to. Dr. Mako isn't here anymore! He went to New York."

Jax jumped all over that. "To the United Nations?"

Stanley seemed genuinely amazed. "Why would he go there?"

"Think, Stanley!" Jax demanded. "What did Mako tell you? It's really important!"

Tommy looked defeated. "Take it easy on the kid, Opus. He honestly doesn't know."

But Jax understood that upsetting Stanley had to come second to stopping Mako and the global Aurora that was just hours away.

He turned on the eight-year-old. "Listen to me, Stanley. Dr. Mako has spread your video worldwide. When nine AM rolls around, hundreds of millions of FreeForAll users are going to grind to a halt. I've seen the damage that can do in one little town. If we're talking about the entire planet, a lot of innocent people will die!"

Stanley set a quivering lip. "You're lying."

"I wish I was," Jax told him. "This is real. Mako is evil."

"He's my cousin and he loves me! He made me better when I got sick!"

"He's not your cousin," Jax insisted. "He only wants you for what you can do. He used me until I saw through him and refused to be a part of it. He tried to kill me, and he'll try to kill you, too, if you cross him."

"No!" Stanley began to cry. "It's not true! You're the one who's evil. I finally have a family, and now you want to trick me out of it! Well, it *won't work*!"

Jax regarded the eight-year-old. He was red-faced and sobbing, almost hysterical. He would never allow himself to be convinced of the truth — not when it meant turning on the sole parent he had ever known.

There was only one way he could reach Stanley. And even that was far from certain. He had never been able to bend this boy. Again and again, Stanley had prevailed — both face-to-face and who knew how many times over FreeForAll.

But now they were out of options and nearly out of time. Jax had no choice but to take him on again. Opus and Sparks versus Arcanov — maybe the greatest confrontation in mesmeric history.

Eyes afire, he rounded on Stanley, muscling right up to the slight boy to make the most of his superior size. Stanley stumbled back at first. But as soon as he realized that their conflict was going to be hypnotic, he wiped away his tears, squared his shoulders, and stood tall. The glance he shot back at Jax was like a physical blow.

Two sets of eyes locked, and the battle was on. The water-down-the-wrong-pipe sensation was almost instantaneous, which both impressed and terrified Jax. He hadn't remembered Stanley being *this* strong.

He's with Mako now, Jax reminded himself. *Learning from the master.*

Jax bore down, concentrating all the centuries of Opus and Sparks heritage on a single point dead center in Stanley's forehead. Agonizingly slowly, he began to see a ghostly picture of himself.

A PIP! he thought triumphantly. *I'm doing it!*

Whether he lost his focus or Stanley just took the initiative away from him, the vision was gone as quickly as it had appeared. Now Stanley had the upper hand, and was pressing in on him, a power drill boring into Jax's mind. He felt himself beginning to relax. . . .

No! You can't! That's how it starts!

He brought up both hands and smacked himself hard in the face. Pain surged through him, especially on the side where Wilson had punched him.

He could hear Tommy asking, "What's going on?" and Kira hushing him. She recognized the mental energy radiating from this mesmeric war, but to Tommy, it must have looked like a couple of guys staring at each other.

The struggle went on without respite, the advantage shifting back and forth between the two combatants. Every time Jax felt himself beginning to penetrate, the eight-year-old would cast him out with a withering counterattack that left Jax gasping. It was at that point that fatigue began to give way to fear. Jax was losing this fight — there was no getting around it. He would not be overpowered by a superior mind-bender. No, this defeat would be more subtle yet just as inevitable. In the past seventy-two hours,

Jax had escaped the army, traversed the country, and participated in a jailbreak. He'd been run ragged, not just physically, but with the overwhelming mental burden of the global tragedy he was trying to prevent. Yes, he was trading blows with Stanley hypnotically. Slowly and surely, though, he was being worn down. He couldn't keep this up. . . .

But how can I give in when there's so much at stake?

"You're very sleepy," Stanley told him.

It was *so* true. The notion of submitting to his fatigue was so tantalizingly tempting that he was listing reasons why he should do it. It made perfect sense. He couldn't fight this any longer. What's more, why would he even want to?

"No!" he rasped aloud.

In the rush of anger at his own weakness, a possible solution came to him. If he couldn't win, maybe he could change the game. The technique had come from Elias Mako himself. He had tricked Jax into performing hypnotism sandwiched between two mirrors. Lost in the infinite reflections, Jax had ended up bending himself. If he could re-create that here, he would have the edge, since he'd experienced such a thing before. Maybe he could keep himself awake and aware while Stanley succumbed and went under.

"Mirrors!" he croaked.

"What?" Tommy demanded.

"Get two mirrors," Jax insisted, striving to keep his voice steady. "Hold them up — one behind him, one behind me."

Kira was baffled. "But why?"

"*Do it!*" Jax commanded.

Kira lifted a large mirror off the wall and rushed to stand in back of Jax, holding it high. "Like this?"

"Another one!"

Tommy raced out into the hall.

"Hurry!" Jax urged, feeling the inexorable tug of Stanley's power.

There was a crash, and Tommy reappeared in short order, bleeding from one hand, lugging an enormous broken piece of mirrored glass. "Seven years of bad luck, Opus," he panted, pushing it along the carpet until it stood behind Stanley. "I hope this is worth it."

Now bracketed between the two mirrors, Jax saw his own reflection repeated to infinity, along with a million diminishing images of Stanley. The eight-year-old was clearly thrown by this, his eyes widening in surprise. His pupils began to shrink down to near pinpoints. His head nodded a little.

Jax took the initiative. "You are very relaxed. . . ." But Stanley wasn't bent — not by him, anyway.

"You okay, Opus?" Tommy hissed. "You're slurring your words."

Not now, Jax tried to reply, but all that came out was a yawn and a gurgle. Across from him, Stanley was very still, the expression on his face stunned. He still didn't seem to be bent, though, as Jax could detect no PIP.

His vision darkening around the edges, Jax watched in amazement as Stanley's eyes rolled back in their sockets and his head slumped forward. *I did it!* Jax cheered, but his celebration was silent. *Okay, get the mirrors away,* he instructed Kira and Tommy. On some level, he was aware that his mouth was not working, but he was too wrapped up in the task at hand now that Stanley was defeated.

Now, what we have to do is —

He never finished the thought, not even in his own head. An enormous burst of acceleration sent him rocketing forward.

30

The mirror images of himself and Stanley blurred to streaks and then winked out entirely, to be replaced by billowing clouds of fiery static. Then a cooling fog.

Where am I?

The scene resolved itself into a suburban backyard — rolling lawn, picket fence, swing set, sandbox. Hamburgers and hot dogs sizzled on a barbecue. Jax stood up for a better view, and understood instantly that something was very different.

I'm too short!

It took a moment for the reality to sink in. He wasn't too short; he was just right — for Stanley. The boosted mesmeric effect of the mirrors had catapulted him into Stanley's mind! This was a scene from Stanley's life! Jax wondered if the same thing had happened to the real Stanley — if the eight-year-old was lost in Jax's memory somewhere. If so, the kid was in for a scary ride.

Sniffling — *so this is what allergies feel like* — he climbed up the ladder and came down the slide facefirst. He was grooving on the sense of speed, until he face-planted on the ground and got a mouthful of grass and earth. Big brother laughed. Little sister clapped her hands and reenacted his hard landing in the sandbox. Mother rushed over and gathered the crying Stanley into her arms —

Wait a minute — Brother? Sister? Parents? But Stanley X was an orphan! The army adopted him from an institution! Who were these people?

A terrible thought occurred to Jax. Was this the family Stanley had *lost*? Was the poor kid the only survivor of a tragic accident? No wonder Stanley was so messed up that even Elias Mako looked good to him.

Still in his mother's arms, Jax-as-Stanley glanced up as if searching for the lightning bolt or meteor that was going to wipe out everybody but him. But the immaculate blue sky showed no lethal projectiles heading for the backyard. The day remained perfect, the aroma of cooking meat tantalizing. Suddenly, Jax knew without having to be told that no calamity was going to overtake this loving group. These people were not fated to die. They had never existed in the first place. The "memory" was not even a memory; it was nothing more than a figment of Stanley's imagination — a lonely orphan conjuring the family he did not and could not have. In a way, it was the saddest scenario of all.

And then the backyard dissolved and Jax was surrounded by static again.

Out of the blizzard, a nasty voice hissed, "No one's ever going to adopt an ugly yellow-eyed loser like you!"

The long white room came into focus around him — twin rows of identical beds. Jax understood that this was an orphanage — Stanley's orphanage. And the oversize bully who stood menacing him was an unpleasant fact of life in this place that was filled with many unpleasant facts of life. A group of smaller boys gathered around to watch the confrontation, most of them grateful that the big kid's attention hadn't fallen on them.

"Nobody likes you, Stupid Stanley." The bully reached down and picked up a large cockroach crawling along the floorboards. "They like this bug better than they like you!"

Holding the roach by an undulating leg, he dangled it over the terrified boy, staring down at him with a cruel leer.

Very few people would have recognized what Jax saw next. As Stanley looked up at the bully, a picture-in-picture image appeared — the cowering Stanley from the big boy's perspective. Jax recognized the PIP — but Stanley didn't!

He has no idea he's a hypnotist!

At least at that moment he didn't.

"Hey — hey!" Anger was overcoming Stanley's fear. "Get that thing away! Shove it up your nose!"

Jax watched in wonder and a little pleased satisfaction as the big boy backed up and stuffed the large insect into his left nostril. There were screams from the other boys. As the scene began to dissolve around him, Jax had the suspicion that this would be the last time Stanley would be bullied in this orphanage.

And then Jax was off again, rolling and tumbling through Stanley's memory. The blizzard of sparks grew

redder, hotter, and Jax had a sense that something important was coming up.

". . . and we're all so thrilled to have found you, Stanley.
We can't wait to welcome you to our family."

The voice made Jax's blood run cold, and the first sight
of its source was even more chilling. Elias Mako's single
black brow and hawk nose gave him a raptor-like appearance. That was exactly what he was — a predator.

Stanley adored him. Jax could feel it. Why not? At
eight years old, Stanley had come to believe that he would
never be adopted. And along came this man called
Ferguson, who later revealed himself to be the infamous
Dr. Mako everyone talked about. But they were all wrong
about him. He wasn't evil; he was just misunderstood. He
was an Arcanov, too — an uncle, or at least a close cousin.
He wanted to use hypnotism to do good in the world!

And he *loved* Stanley. The kid was sure of it. Soon he
would meet the rest of his cousins. He had a family after
all — a big one. There would be Thanksgivings and get-
togethers and movies and ballgames and fireworks on the
Fourth of July. He'd go to a regular school and have friends
and do things that normal people did! After eight long
years, it was finally happening for Stanley X — Stanley
Ferguson — Stanley *Mako*.

There was just one little detail they had to take care
of first before all that great family stuff could kick in.
Nothing too complicated — Stanley had to record a
short video that would help clear his cousin's legal prob-
lems and set the world right. It was to be a hypnotic clip,

with him looking into the camera as if mesmerizing a subject.

And then Jax was doing it, saying the words from the FreeForAll video, speaking in Stanley's young voice as Mako ran the camera.

"You will stay perfectly still until you hear this special word — the name of what I'm holding in my hand right now. Remember it well. . . ."

Panicked that the memory would fade out and he would lose this vital moment, Jax glanced down at his palm to see what was there. It was a large porcelain dragonfly.

Dragonfly. That was the trigger word that would shut down Mako's global Aurora.

The word that could save the world.

I've got to get out of here! I've got to break the connection!

But he could already see the gale of static swirling all around him, closing in on him, carrying him to another place inside Stanley's mind.

You can't forget it! he exhorted himself. *No matter what happens. Dragonfly, dragonfly, dragonfly . . .*

He kept on repeating the word as he waited for the next memory to coalesce around him.

It never came — not the location, anyway. Instead, he was flattened by paralyzing pain, overwhelming nausea, and blindness.

No, not blindness. Stanley wasn't seeing *nothing*; he was seeing *everything* — millions of images all at the same time. That was when Jax recognized this for what it was —

hypnotic blowback! *Stanley's* blowback from the mesmeric message that was being spread across the entire world.

What Jax had experienced from the original Operation Aurora paled in comparison. That had come from several hundred people — few enough that he'd been able to make out individual PIP images. This had to be coming from millions!

He felt his strength ebbing, a numbness setting in.

It's going to kill me!

A more rational thought: How could it kill him? It hadn't killed Stanley. He recalled the boy's words: *He's my cousin and he loves me! He made me better when I got sick!*

That's what the poor kid was talking about — this terrible blowback!

But to save Stanley, all Mako had to do was to pull the message off FreeForAll. *This* blowback was coming from Stanley's memory. It could go on forever!

The kaleidoscope of PIP images began to recede from him until he was surrounded by glaring light, staring at a point of utter blackness in the distance. All at once, the dot shattered, and he was hurtling through space and time, falling faster and faster until he, too, winked out of existence.

31

The screams were raw, like animal cries, and came at exactly the same moment. Jax and Stanley, squared off opposite each other, both crumpled first to their knees and then to the floor, where they lay, gasping.

"Let's get rid of the mirrors!" Kira ordered, turning hers to face the wall.

Tommy dropped his, breaking it into countless pieces. He crunched through the shards and hauled Jax to his feet. "Opus — wake up!"

Kira saw to the fallen Stanley, supporting his head with one hand and patting his cheek with the other. Wilson, still bent, looked on blandly. It wasn't that he couldn't see the events in the room, but between the post-hypnotic suggestions implanted by Mako and Jax's clashing commands, he was a blank slate.

Tommy turned desperate eyes on Kira. "Why aren't they waking up? Who hypnotized who?"

She shook her head helplessly. "I have no experience with this. They might have hypnotized each other."

"What should we do?" Tommy persisted.

"What can we do?" she replied. "We wait for them to come out of it."

"But what if they never do?"

"They have to," she said, not as confidently as she would have liked. "Whatever happened to them, it was purely mental —"

"Don't give me your freaky mumbo jumbo!" He turned to Jax's inert form. "Don't you dare leave me, man! Don't even *think* about it! I drove a bulldozer into a police station for you! In New Jersey!"

Jax opened one eye. "What do you want — a medal?"

"Opus!"

Tommy was so overjoyed that he dropped Jax. The jolt to the floor brought Stanley back. The boy sat up in Kira's arms, gurgling and spitting as if he'd just been rescued from drowning.

"Don't be scared," Kira comforted him. "We won't hurt you."

Stanley was practically hysterical. "It's my fault! All those people are going to die — because of *me*!"

Light dawned on Jax. Just as he had been wandering inside Stanley's memory, Stanley had been wandering inside his!

"What did you see?" he asked.

"Dr. Mako lied to me," Stanley quavered. "He's not a good person! He tried to kill you and your family. And he made me record that message! And now — and now —"

"It hasn't happened yet," Jax cut him off. "Maybe we can prevent it."

"We *can't*!" Stanley wailed. "Nobody can, not even Dr. Mako! It's in too many people's heads! At nine o'clock, everybody who got my message will just stop!"

"Listen, Stanley. Just like you were in my mind, I was in yours. The trigger word to reverse the suggestion is *dragonfly*, isn't it?"

Stanley nodded. "But there's no way we could ever deliver it to the whole world!"

"There *is* one way," Jax countered. "And you know who showed it to us? Mako himself."

"Mako?" Tommy echoed. "He doesn't strike me as the helpful type."

"Mako scheduled the post-hypnotic suggestion for nine o'clock this morning — exactly when the big UN conference is scheduled. The opening ceremony is supposed to have the largest TV and Internet audience the world has ever known."

"So," concluded Kira breathlessly, "if we can bend our way to the podium and deliver the trigger word exactly at nine o'clock, we can undo the damage the minute it starts."

Jax nodded. "We can't save everybody, but we might be able to reach enough people that they can rescue the rest."

"But that's in New York!" Tommy exclaimed. "It's almost two in the morning. Do the buses run this late?"

"We'll have to call a taxi," Jax decided.

"Have we got enough cash for that?" asked Tommy. "It's going to cost a fortune to drive to Manhattan from here."

"Money's no object," Jax said solemnly. "However much it costs, that's how much the driver is going to think we're giving him. Maybe we can find a way to make sure he gets paid after all this is over."

Kira nodded. "I agree. Stopping Mako is more important than anything else." She pulled out her phone and began tapping the screen. "Here it is — Pine Bough Taxi. Let's hope they answer their phone at night."

The car was unmarked except for the license plate: G — 0745. The *G* stood for *government.* It was after two AM when it pulled up in front of the Pine Bough police station and the uniformed military officers got out.

Colonel Brassmeyer squinted through the darkness at the small building with the shattered doorway. "What hit this place?"

"More than hypnotism, that's for sure," commented his companion, Captain Pedroia.

Inside, the devastation was even worse. The desks were toothpicks; filing cabinets lay on their sides, bleeding papers; the bars of the holding cell were knocked off and bent. In the center of the ruined office sat the Bobcat, its digger askew.

"Jackson Opus did *this*?" Brassmeyer asked the police chief.

The older man shook his head. "He had help. He and the girl were in custody. It was the other boy who brought in the Bobcat and busted up the place."

"Any sign of the kids?" Pedroia probed.

"Patrolman Wisnewski said he didn't notice anything. Where exactly were you driving, Wisnewski?"

The young officer looked completely blank. "I — I can't remember. . . ."

His boss stared at him. "What do you mean, you can't remember? That doesn't make any sense!"

Brassmeyer and Pedroia exchanged a knowing glance.

"Actually," said the captain, "it makes all the sense in the world." The HoWaRD officers had not spent the past months working with mind-benders without learning how to recognize the aftereffects of hypnotic manipulation.

"Well, would you mind letting me in on it?" the chief asked in exasperation. "I've had a rough night."

"It's classified," Brassmeyer informed him.

Pedroia spoke up. "Has your squad car got one of those cameras on it? The kind that records everywhere you've been?"

32

The crunching of tires on the gravel drive of the Quackenbush property came earlier than Jax had expected.

"That was fast," noted Kira. "The taxi company said half an hour."

"What should we do about him?" asked Tommy, indicating Wilson.

The burly teen, still bent, was lying on the couch, totally focused on the broken TV and Stanley's cartoons. Jax walked over and stared into his enemy's eyes. "Wilson, we were never here. You're holding the fort, and Stanley's upstairs, asleep. You will remember none of this when you wake up in the morning — you know, if there's a morning to wake up to."

"It might be easier that way," Tommy mourned. "There's no way I'll ever be able to explain all this to my folks."

They ran out of the house and started in the direction of the long drive.

Kira said it aloud just as Jax registered the same observation. "That doesn't look like a taxi."

About a hundred yards away, the car stopped and a

passenger climbed out. It was too dark to see the face, but there was no mistaking the uniform. An eagle on the collar winked in the distant light from the house.

"Brassmeyer!" Jax almost choked over the name.

"Who's that?" Tommy whispered.

And then the army officer's finger was pointing in their direction. *"Opus!"*

Jax, Stanley, Kira, and Tommy fled, running around the side of the house. Brassmeyer and Pedroia sprinted after them.

"Why are we running?" panted Kira. "If we just explain what we're doing, they'll help us!"

"You don't know the army," Jax rasped. "Yeah, they'll help us — in six months when they sort it all out! We need to go *now*!"

"But we'll never get our taxi with two guys chasing us!" Tommy lamented. "How are we going to make it to the city?"

A loud whinny came from the darkness ahead of them.

"The stable!" Kira exclaimed.

"We can't hide!" Jax declared. "We have to get to New York!"

"And we will," Kira promised. "On horseback."

"It's twenty miles!" Jax protested.

"I used to ride that far every weekend. We can do this." She added, "Anyway, have you got a better idea?"

The two officers pounded through the darkness after the four fleeing young figures. The army required them to be in good shape. But the Hypnotic Warfare Research Department hadn't offered much opportunity for physical training.

They rounded the corner of the house and pulled up, squinting through the gloom.

"Where'd they go?" panted the colonel.

Pedroia, too, was out of breath. "The little guy — was that *Stanley*? What's he doing here?"

"They can't be far," reasoned Brassmeyer with military singleness of purpose.

They resumed pursuit, this time at a jog, their eyes sweeping the property. Suddenly, a shadowy form exploded from the barn and fled directly across their line of vision.

"There!" barked the colonel.

The officers gave chase, but their quarry was fast and agile, and kept well ahead of them. The boy led them to the back of the house and kept on going, clear around the building toward the front again.

"Give it up, Opus!" rasped Brassmeyer.

"Come on, Jax!" added Pedroia. "We're not your enemies!"

The two men were exhausted, their breath coming out in gasps, but they were closing the gap.

"Is it just me," the psychiatrist heaved, "or is he slowing down on purpose?"

"Doesn't matter!" Brassmeyer spat. He reached out, grabbed the fleeing figure by one arm, and spun him around. "Very stupid, Opus —"

The stunned officer found himself face-to-face with Tommy Cicerelli.

"Where's Jax?" demanded Pedroia.

As if on cue, the stable door burst open and out shot a magnificent black stallion at a full gallop. It carried three riders — Kira at the reins, the slight Stanley in the middle, and Jax bringing up the rear. The animal ran a half lap of its practice track then leaped the fence and disappeared across the field into the night.

Brassmeyer rounded on Tommy. "Tell me I didn't see what I just saw."

"Don't blame Jax," Tommy said urgently. "He's trying to save the world."

"What does the world need to be saved *from*?" Pedroia probed.

"How should I know?" Tommy howled. "I don't understand any of this stuff! I'm not even a hypnotist!"

"Where are they going on that horse?" Brassmeyer growled.

Tommy bit his lip. He wasn't sure if Jax, Kira, and Stanley were going to make it to the UN on time. But if there was a chance they might, *nothing* could be allowed to interfere with their mission there.

The colonel took hold of Tommy by the scruff of the collar and began to drag him to the car. "All right, smart guy. You're coming with us."

"Okay," said Tommy. "But there's another kid in the house, you know. Wilson somebody."

"DeVries?!" Pedroia exclaimed in surprise.

"I think so. Big guy. Jax bent him so hard he won't wake up till Christmas."

The two officers exchanged a helpless look. Jackson Opus, Stanley X, and now Wilson. What had brought these HoWaRDs together in this place?

As always, Brassmeyer made the decision. "Find DeVries and see what you can squeeze out of him." He began to frog-march Tommy toward the car. "I'll keep this one with me. We've got a horse to catch."

If anything less had been at stake, Jax would have called the whole thing off.

He clung to Kira's midsection like a drowning man to a life preserver. Stanley sat squashed between them, too frightened to utter a complaint. Jax was even more scared than Stanley, but if he loosened his grip, he was sure to fly off and be dashed to pieces on the ground. Not to mention that he was probably the only reason Stanley wasn't launched into outer space.

Kira didn't seem to notice the raw terror that existed behind her. She was a brilliant rider, completely focused on her mount and the path that lay ahead. A billionaire's stable raised no ordinary horses. The stallion's stall proclaimed him to be named Black Quack, with bloodlines leading back to two Kentucky Derby winners. They were riding on the horse equivalent of Jax himself — the nexus of two great families.

"Just because he's a racehorse doesn't mean you have to

race him!" Jax shouted in the direction of Kira's ear. "If Stanley and I fall off, then where will we be?"

Kira just laughed. "This is *slow*! He's used to a level track, not cross-country in the dark!"

They continued across endless fields, Kira lighting the way through the darkest parts with the flashlight app on her phone. After a few miles, the pastureland ended, and a heavily treed area began. Skillfully, Kira pulled back on the reins, slowing Black Quack to a walk as they searched for another way to New York. Eventually, they ran into a narrow two-lane road heading east, trotting through a little town, the stores and restaurants darkened and closed up for the night.

Stanley yawned. "Is New York very far away?"

"Not really," Jax told him. "See that glow in the sky — that's from the city lights. But these roads are really winding, so it's hard to know where you're going."

"Use the GPS in your phone," Kira advised.

"Are you kidding?" Jax complained. "If I let go even with one finger, I'll be five miles behind you before you even notice I'm missing."

"Fine — I'll navigate. But you guys have to be the headlight."

In the end, Stanley, who was wedged in place, held up Jax's phone in flashlight mode while Kira followed GPS directions. It was fine until the eight-year-old nodded off from the rocking motion of the horse. Jax had to take over, clinging to the phone, Kira, and the slumbering

Stanley, while squeezing Black Quack's flanks with both knees. It was an awful position to maintain as the hours dragged on.

But not half as awful as the consequences if we can't get to the UN in time.

33

In the little cottage in the residential section of Fort Calhoun, Monica Opus was shaken out of a deep sleep to find her husband staring down at her.

"Monica — you up?"

"I am now," she murmured. "Something on your mind?"

To her amazement, a sob escaped him.

"Ashton — what's wrong?"

"What kind of parents are we?" he moaned.

She folded her pillow and propped herself on it. "Jax is fine. Captain Pedroia said he's in New Jersey and he'll be home soon."

"I know," her husband agreed. "It makes perfect sense. The question is — *should* it make sense? Shouldn't it bother us that our twelve-year-old son is in a jail cell fifteen hundred miles away?"

"There's no reason for us to go looking for him," she droned automatically. "We have to stay here at Fort Calhoun and let the army protect us. That's the most important thing." The language was almost identical to the mesmeric message Jax had implanted in his parents before leaving the post.

Of course, they had no memory of that.

Mr. Opus sighed. "I think so, too. I'm totally sure Jax is okay, and we have nothing to worry about. The part that bugs me is" — he looked haunted — "*why* we feel that way."

"Ashton?"

"Why do we think everything is hunky-dory when any other parents in our place would be freaking out?"

She frowned at him. "I'm not following you."

"Monica, when I was growing up, I was the only kid who loved eating his vegetables, the only kid who did his household chores not because he *had* to, but because he honestly *enjoyed* them. At least, I thought I did. In reality, I was the perfect son because I had *help*."

At last, Mrs. Opus clued in. "You think the reason we're not more concerned about Jax is he *hypnotized* us?" she asked incredulously.

Her husband nodded. "I think he was trying to spare us the heartache. And now he's in trouble halfway across the country and we can't get to him."

She looked alarmed. "I hear what you're telling me, and I *still* can't bring myself to be upset about it. I understand that Jax needs us, but for some reason I can't make myself believe it's a big deal."

"That's the hypnotism talking!" Mr. Opus said breathlessly.

She threw off the blankets. "We've got to get to New Jersey!"

Her husband switched on the light, grabbed his phone

from the nightstand, and began tapping at the screen. "There's a five thirty flight to New York from Oklahoma City. If we hurry, we can be on it!"

It was shortly after five AM when Jax noticed he was no longer looking at the familiar glow of the city. Sheer panic — were they off course? Had they gotten turned around somehow? Then he realized that a different glow surrounded them now — dawn was coming.

Kira steered Black Quack onto a larger road, keeping to the shoulder past diners and gas stations that were preparing for the new day. To their left, the occasional car whizzed by. It was amazing how early the signs and sounds of life began.

And then a half-demented voice hollered, "Get lost, Opus, we're coming up on you!"

Jax wheeled around, nearly dislodging himself from his perch. Tommy hung halfway out the window of a dark sedan directly behind them.

"Quiet, you!" The driver, Colonel Brassmeyer, reached over and yanked Tommy back into the car.

"Kira —"

She didn't have to be told. "Hang on!" And they were off, scrambling down a low embankment, leaping a ditch, and galloping through a 7-Eleven parking lot to an inner service road. Brassmeyer took the next exit and roared off behind them. He gunned the engine, and the car pulled even with Black Quack.

When racing, the big stallion always wore blinders, so he wasn't used to the sight of a challenger running beside him. Black Quack took this personally; he was accustomed to being first. The animal mustered every ounce of speed he'd been trained to keep under tight control and blasted across the field like a rocket. The colonel stomped on the gas, watching in amazement as the horse continued to pull away, even as the speedometer approached seventy. There was a very Western *"Giddyap!"* that could only have come from Tommy's throat.

It was almost too late when Brassmeyer noticed a garbage truck backing out of the lane directly ahead of them. Not since basic training had he strained himself physically as hard as he did when he jammed on the brakes. The sedan fishtailed, spun around, and skidded to a halt inches from the truck. There was a loud pop as the left rear tire blew.

HoWaRD's commander jumped from the car just in time to see the horse and riders disappear into the early-morning mist. He knew enough about tactics to understand that he was out of this operation. From here on, it was up to local law enforcement.

How hard could it be to find three kids on a stolen racehorse?

34

It was a rare sight in New Jersey, or anywhere else for that matter — a squad car pulling over a horse.

It happened shortly after six thirty in the town of Clifton, just east of the Garden State Parkway.

"All right, you three," the officer said sternly. "Come down from there."

He looked up into the eyes of three powerful mind-benders and never knew what hit him. Thrown by the intensity of Kira's luminous baby blues, he bounced to Jax's burning violet stare, and finally to the wide, open amber gaze of what appeared to be an innocent child.

"You are calm . . . relaxed. . . ." Stanley commanded in a very young voice that nonetheless dripped with author-ity. "You're not even thinking about that big gun in your holster." He peered at Jax through the corner of his eye. "What now?"

"Tell him to get back in the car and lead us to the Lincoln Tunnel," Jax decided. "No other cop will arrest us if we've got a police escort."

So it was that Black Quack and his three passengers trotted behind the squad car clear through the heart of suburban New Jersey. They passed MetLife Stadium and crossed the canal into Secaucus. The majestic stallion caused quite a stir in rush-hour traffic, but the other motorists assumed that the black-and-white in front of them, flashers whirling, meant that the young equestrians had special permission to be there. And to police officers who'd received the APB on three kids on horseback, they appeared to be already in custody.

The squad car escorted them through the streets of Union City, under the high looping roadway known as the Helix, and right up to the bottleneck of traffic converging on the Lincoln Tunnel. The hypnotized trooper blurped his siren and drove onto the shoulder, Black Quack trotting calmly behind him. Cruiser and horse ignored the toll plaza and bypassed a long line of vehicles that led to the mouth of the tunnel. Here, dozens of lanes squeezed down to six, and even a squad car had to wait its turn.

Jax frowned at the large police presence at the entrance, monitoring the traffic creeping into the tunnel. There had to be twenty officers, most of them peering suspiciously at the black stallion and its three riders. Confused questions were shouted back and forth and spoken into walkie-talkies.

We could bend some of them, but not all.

He checked his watch. It was almost eight — barely an hour before the unthinkable was scheduled to happen. It was getting to be crunch time.

He leaned over to Kira. "Floor it."

It was undoubtedly the wrong phrase — a horse had no gas pedal. Kira, though, understood immediately. "Hold on tight," she advised.

And then they were cantering through the stopped vehicles, side mirrors passing mere inches from the horse's flanks. Black Quack danced between eighteen-wheelers, buses, SUVs, taxis, and cars of all shapes and sizes. The stallion's footwork was delicate, yet sure, and rock solid on the pavement. He moved with deliberate care, yet covered a remarkable amount of distance very quickly. By the time the tunnel officers rushed to block the way, Black Quack was already behind them, tracing a path through the rush-hour crush. And since the tube was already clogged with cars, the only way to give chase was on foot.

"Are we allowed to be doing this?" Stanley wondered as they trotted between the astounded motorists.

"Did you see any sign back there that said 'No Horses'?" Jax asked him.

Kira's attention was focused on the irregular lane created by the gap between the two lanes of vehicles. "Just be ready to start hypnotizing on the other side. I have a feeling the cops are going to be waiting for us."

Jax swallowed hard. They'd done an amazing job making it this far, but the worst was yet to come. They had just tweaked the beard of the NYPD — the largest police force in the world, already on high alert because of the UN conference.

The farther they made it through the mile-and-a-half-long tunnel, the louder came the chorus of car horns and shouts to speed them on their way.

"Get off the road!"

"What are you — nuts?"

"That's one way to beat the traffic!"

"Curse you and the horse you rode in on!"

The noise spooked Black Quack, and Kira hunched over the racehorse's neck, speaking soothing words to calm him.

They cantered past the state line dividing New Jersey and New York, signifying the home stretch. It was there that Black Quack began to detect light coming in from the end of the tunnel and picked up his pace.

As they burst out of the tube, the stallion saw open pavement and made for it. There was an enormous traffic jam at street level, most of it caused by the police, who were setting up a roadblock to intercept the horse and its three riders. Several officers watched in openmouthed wonder as Black Quack soared over the blue-painted saw-horses and clattered up West Forty-First Street. The roadways were choked with cars, so the thoroughbred galloped onto the sidewalk, scattering pedestrians as he went.

As they approached Ninth Avenue, Black Quack reared up in fear at the rushing river of downtown traffic crossing in front of him.

Kira clung to the reins, struggling for control. "Easy, boy!"

But the horse became even more agitated as a police car pulled over to the curb, siren blaring.

The cop was already speaking into his walkie-talkie as he jumped out. "Found 'em, corner of —"

That was as far as he got. Jax bent him with a single scorching glance. "Tell them it was a false alarm," he instructed. "And stop the cars on Ninth so we can cross."

They continued east, traversing the city. As they passed just south of Times Square, Jax caught a glimpse of the huge video billboard. It showed a live feed from the General Assembly chamber of the UN, where the historic conference was set to begin in — when he saw the time, he nearly gagged on his own heart, which jumped up into his throat — *forty-three minutes*!

As they galloped on, Jax kept an eye on his watch, agonizing as the time slipped away. 8:21 . . . 8:32 . . . 8:43 . . .

"We're not going to make it!" Stanley moaned.

"Don't say that!" Kira shot back through gritted teeth. Up ahead, she spotted three helmeted cops on horseback, members of the NYPD mounted unit. "Follow my lead," she called over her shoulder.

"Not them!" Jax exclaimed. "They can chase us anywhere!"

Undaunted, Kira pulled the big stallion alongside the trio. She locked eyes with the first officer, hypnotizing him quickly. Jax and Stanley clued in and took care of the other two. Moments later, there were four horses galloping across Manhattan, stopping traffic as they crossed the avenues. As they made their way to the east side, several more cops on horseback joined their procession, only to be mesmerized by the three young mind-benders. By the time the group reached the heavily guarded United Nations complex on First Avenue, Black Quack and his riders were invisible at the center of the cluster of mounted police officers.

Jax checked his watch. 8:51.

"Nine minutes!" he hissed.

From the midst of the mounted unit exploded Black Quack, bearing his three riders. The length of his stride and the grace and sheer power of his movement proclaimed that this was much more than an ordinary police mount. He cleared the barriers and closed the distance to the UN entrance before anyone could take a step in his direction. Haughty and magnificent, he streaked past the fluttering flags of one hundred ninety-three member states and discharged his young passengers just under the wire.

Armed security guards ran to block their way. But the three newcomers were thoroughbreds of a different variety, wielding mesmeric powers that even few hypnotists could match. They bent them all, one at a time, leaving them dancing, sitting cross-legged on the carpet, jogging in place, conducting an imaginary symphony, doing push-ups — anything that came to mind in this mad rush. They worked with a speed and efficiency that was nothing short of amazing.

No, thought Jax. *Not amazing. Desperate.*

8:56.

Free at last, the three sprinted down the marble corridor and burst into the General Assembly. At the sight of the vast, soaring chamber, with its towering gold monolith, Jax took a small step backward, stomping on Stanley's toe.

"Ow!" hissed the eight-year-old in a hushed tone.

Every seat was full, every delegation complete. Jax recognized faces he'd only seen in newspapers or on TV — presidents, prime ministers, kings. How could he expect to be heard in this place where every other voice represented an entire country?

But none of them can stop what's about to happen!

As the three ran down the side aisle, the secretary-general himself rose and approached the podium. He paused, waiting for the chamber to come to order, and was joined by someone else — a tall man with a hawk nose and burning eyes under a single black brow.

Elias Mako.

35

The two men spoke briefly. After their conversation, the secretary-general backed away, and it was Dr. Mako who climbed the green-carpeted stairs to the dais.

Mako bent the secretary-general of the United Nations!

Jax, Stanley, and Kira reached the foot of the rostrum just as Mako stepped to the microphone. A security guard blocked their way, his hand on the butt of his pistol.

Kira fixed the man with an intense stare, mesmerizing him quickly. "You are eating M&M's using chopsticks."

Instantly, the hand left the weapon, manipulating invisible sticks in the air.

That was when Mako looked down and saw the three young mind-benders at the foot of the stairs. It was 8:58. Two minutes from now, the world would be an unrecognizable place. This was literally their last chance.

Knowing there was no other way — knowing it was a horrible risk — Jax met the terrifying gaze of his former mentor. Never before had he been able to hypnotize Elias Mako, but maybe things were different now. They *had* to be.

The instant their eyes locked, Jax felt the jolt of the man's strength. It wasn't just the power — Mako himself had admitted that the talent Jax had inherited from his Opus and Sparks ancestry was probably stronger. But the experience and sheer ruthlessness of the man could overwhelm even a greater natural gift. He wielded mesmeric ability the way a great warrior handled a sword or battle ax — the weapon didn't have to be special for him to cut you to pieces.

Jax mustered every microvolt of hypnotic attack that was left inside him after a sleepless night on horseback and hurled it at Elias Mako. The man flinched as if he'd been struck. Jax pressed his advantage, his face distorted with the depth of his effort.

Their minds locked — the irresistible force and the immovable object, a monumental struggle of might against might.

Jax experienced a ray of hope. Was that a PIP? Or was it the hallucination of someone who needed to see one, and needed it badly?

And then the PIP was there — for real — and Jax had won. He'd done it. He'd overpowered the founder of Sentia — and just in the nick of time.

"You are very relaxed. . . ." he began.

"I believe you have that backward," came Mako's quiet voice from above him.

It happened with the swiftness of a cobra strike. The picture-in-picture image was gone and a sharp-toothed carnivore was tearing away the layers of protection around Jax's brain. In terrified awe, he realized that he'd fallen into a mesmeric trap. Mako had allowed him partway into his mind, baiting Jax into letting down his defenses. And the beast had pounced.

Fueled by panic, he struggled to extricate himself, but only seemed to fall further under his adversary's control.

"It is you who is relaxed," Mako said in a soothing tone.

No! Jax intended to scream it out loud, but for some reason, his brain wasn't connected to his tongue. Or maybe he'd simply changed his mind. What was so bad, after all? He *was* relaxed. In fact, he felt fantastic. He couldn't imagine why he'd ever thought Elias Mako was the enemy. Mako was his teacher and his friend, the person who had discovered and nurtured Jax's talent. Whatever this kind man was doing, he had Jax's best interests at heart.

"The only thing that will make you feel even more wonderful," Mako went on in a mellow tone, "is to take the pistol from that security man, hold it to your temple, and squeeze the trigger."

Nothing had ever seemed more reasonable to Jackson Opus. He was on his way to a perfect, blissful state. There was just one little task he had to perform first. . . .

He reached for the holster and put his hand on the grip of the gun.

Horrified, both Kira and Stanley seized Jax's hand, keeping it away from the weapon. But Jax seemed absolutely determined to grab the pistol. The guard continued to manipulate his unseen chopsticks, completely unaware of the three-way tug-of-war for his sidearm.

"Is he crazy?" Stanley panted. "What's he doing?"

"He's not crazy; he's *bent*," grunted Kira. "Mako's trying to kill him!"

Enraged, Stanley let go of Jax's hand, ran out, and interposed himself in the sight line between Mako and Jax. He glared up at the only parent he'd ever known, packing all the hypnotic punch of the mysterious Arcanovs, mixed with his own personal anger.

Mako staggered back. It was taking most of his mental energy to maintain his hold on Jax. He had nothing left for this eight-year-old powerhouse. It snapped the mesmeric link with Jax, who stumbled briefly. Kira steadied him.

A murmur began in the General Assembly. Of course, none of the three thousand delegates were aware of the titanic hypnotic struggle in progress at the front of the chamber. They were simply wondering why this speaker hadn't picked up the gavel to begin the historic session.

Reeling, Jax caught a glimpse of a digital time readout. The glowing chronometer was at 8:59:24. He ran to Stanley and spun the boy around.

"I can beat him!" Stanley hissed.

"You can't," Jax said urgently. "But together, maybe the two of us can."

Stanley stared at him in bewilderment.

"Back at the horse farm, we were in each other's minds!" Jax fumbled to put his plan into words. "We have to combine our power like that — and turn it on him!"

Their eyes fell into synch in a connection that all but crackled with electricity. It was the second confrontation of these two minds, each carrying its centuries of mesmeric ability. Yet there was something very different about this moment. At the farm they had been opponents, and their conflict had driven each into the dark memories of the other. But here they were united toward a single, crystal-clear purpose.

For Jax, the General Assembly winked out for an instant. He sensed, rather than saw, two orbs of pure energy colliding. The merging was violent — explosion, eruption, flares of white heat. But when it was over, the pool that remained pulsated with limitless power.

"Now!" exclaimed Jax.

Moving as one, he and Stanley climbed the stairs and unleashed on their nemesis the greatest reservoir of mesmeric force that had ever existed. Jax was aware of a rapid-fire detonation of hundreds of images. It was almost like blowback. When he was finally able to identify it, the truth was nearly as shocking as the event itself. He had experienced, in a few blazing seconds, the entire life of Elias Mako from birth till now. It was as if they had opened his mind and sucked out the contents.

Mako wobbled for a second and crumpled to the floor, boneless.

Jax jumped over his enemy's unmoving form and reached for the microphone. As he grasped it, he caught a glimpse of the chronometer just as 8:59:59 changed to 9:00:00.

Halfway through the most important action he would ever take, Jackson Opus stopped. So did fully half the delegates in the General Assembly. Outside, on the streets of New York, life ground to a halt. Around the world, hundreds of millions of people were suddenly frozen in time. The worldwide catastrophe he'd nearly died trying to prevent was happening.

Jax understood none of it. He was perfectly content as he stood motionless, obeying the post-hypnotic suggestion from FreeForAll. He did not think about the trains thundering into stations, their engineers bent and shut down; the ships with no captains; the cars and trucks with no drivers. He did not consider the patients waiting for doctors who would not be coming; the babies screaming for parents who could not hear them. Mammoth power plants operated without oversight; large factories were unmanned. Soon the accidents would start — the explosions, meltdowns, fires, floods. Every pot on every burner in every home on earth was a potential inferno. Yet the police or firefighters or first responders would be just as incapacitated as the rest.

Jax was oblivious to it all. He knew only the mindless calm contentment of someone following a mesmeric command.

And then an eight-year-old voice beside him howled, *"Dragonfly!"* and life began again.

When the General Assembly reappeared around Jax, the chronometer read 9:00:04. So the global Aurora was on — *but only four seconds in!* There was still a chance to undo this before the damage got out of hand. He himself was living proof of that. Stanley had brought him back with a single word.

He looked out into the ocean of TV and video cameras, microphones, handheld devices, and recorders. It was supposedly the largest media audience ever. Jax sure hoped so. The message he had was short, but it needed to get to every corner of the globe.

"Dragonfly!" he bellowed. *"Dragonfly! Dragonfly! Dragonfly!"*

Beside him, Stanley joined in the chorus. The battery of UN interpreters translated the word into every language known to humankind.

It wasn't enough, not nearly. What about people walking on streets, sleeping, out of range of media? Who would save them? He could never do it himself. The task was too enormous — every bit as vast as the awful abuse of hypnotism that had started this mess in the first place.

All at once, he had the answer.

He stared out into the cameras into the widest audience in history. "Relax and look into my eyes. . . . Do it now. . . . Nothing has ever been so important. Say 'dragonfly.' Shout it out loud. Scream it from your windows and rooftops. Bellow it through bullhorns and loudspeakers. Wake up your neighbors, your friends, total strangers. Don't stop until everyone around you is awake and well!"

He fell back, exhausted, pushing Stanley up to his place at the microphone. Stanley began his own version of the hypnotic message in an attempt to reach anyone Jax might have missed. By the time *he* was finished, cries of "Dragonfly!" were ringing out all over the General Assembly. Reporters, delegates, and heads of state joined together to spread the magic word.

Kira ran up to join them on the podium, her face pale with dread. "Do you think it worked?"

Jax looked around. "It worked in here. But here isn't the whole world. We have to check outside."

Stanley's eyes traveled to the fallen Mako. "Is he dead?" he asked in a small voice.

"He's still breathing," Kira observed, "but that's about it."

"Leave him for the police," Jax said dismissively. "I hope they give him all the care and compassion that he gave us. Come on, let's see what kind of shape the city's in."

They retraced their steps out of the chamber, raced up the corridor to the exit, and stopped short, horrified, under the flags of one hundred ninety-three nations.

"Oh my God!" breathed Kira.

36

In the minutes before nine AM, Flight 865 circled low over the New York metropolitan sprawl.

"Good morning, passengers," came the captain's voice over the PA system. *"We've begun our descent into New York's LaGuardia Airport. . . ."*

In row 22, Monica Opus turned to her husband. "I still feel silly about this. I'm sure Jax is absolutely fine."

"I'm sure, too," he agreed, a little too loudly, since all sound was muffled by his headphones. "And I'm also sure we can't trust that feeling."

He returned his attention to the Direct TV screen in front of him. He was watching the big UN conference, which seemed to be off to a disorganized start. The secretary-general had backed off, and another man was at the podium. He looked vaguely familiar, but the camera wasn't close on him. It was following some kind of disturbance off to the side. . . .

Suddenly, Mr. Opus grabbed his wife's arm and directed her attention to the small screen. "Monica — isn't that *Mako?*"

But before she could confirm the identification, the

man at the podium crumpled to the floor. Two boys scrambled up to take his place at the microphone.

"Jax?!" chorused the Opuses.

The captain's voice cut in again as they felt the landing gear deploy. *"Ladies and gentlemen, air traffic control has cleared us to begin our final approach at exactly nine AM, which is right about —"*

There was dead silence from the cockpit, but the Opuses wouldn't have noticed anyway. Neither would most of the passengers. Nine o'clock had arrived, and three-quarters of the people on the plane had stopped dead — including Ashton and Monica Opus and both pilots.

In the cockpit, the controls slipped out of the captain's lifeless fingers, and Flight 865 began a sharp descent toward the New York City skyline. A handful of passengers cried out in dismay at the drastic drop, but most of them remained unmoving and unmoved, responding to Stanley's post-hypnotic suggestion.

Through his headphones, Ashton Opus heard a single word: *"Dragonfly!"* He awoke with a start into a scene of pure panic. Screams rang out around him. Yet most of the passengers and crew — including Monica — were frozen. The plane was in a steep dive. Through the window, Manhattan was at a forty-five-degree angle and coming up fast. Who was flying this thing?

The stark answer: nobody. Beyond the cockpit door, the pilots were out of commission as their aircraft screamed toward the ground.

And suddenly, Jax was close-up on the seat-back screen. What was he saying?

"Relax and look into my eyes. . . . Do it now. . . . Nothing has ever been so important. . . ."

Mr. Opus was instantly captured by the mesmeric message. "Dragonfly!" he bellowed at the top of his lungs.

Throughout the cabin, everyone who'd been watching the UN took up the call. The trigger word brought dozens of passengers and crew back to themselves.

They awoke to a plane that was in a suicide plunge. Oxygen masks clattered down from above.

"Ashton?" Mrs. Opus's voice was full of terror.

The man who had been manipulated by hypnotic commands his whole life seemed to understand that this one was a matter of life and death. He leaped out of his seat and barreled up the aisle, bellowing "Dragonfly!" all the way.

Three flight attendants rushed to intercept him. He plowed right through them and began pounding on the entrance to the cockpit.

"Dragonfly! *Dragonfly!!*"

On the other side of the armored door, his howls reached the ears of the copilot. The trigger word startled him into a reality straight out of his wildest nightmares: New York City, hurtling up at him at terminal velocity. *The nose of the plane was on a collision course with the United Nations!*

He grabbed the controls and yanked with all his might.

The plane shuddered and did not respond. A commercial airliner was not built for stunt flying.

He hung on because there was nothing else to do, pulling hard until sweat poured from his brow. He was close enough to make out the gravel on the UN roof.

Flight 865 was going down.

Tommy was in the cab of a tow truck, squeezed in between Brassmeyer and the driver, when nine AM hit. The driver went limp. His hands left the wheel and his head lolled back against the seat.

Moving at thirty miles per hour, with Brassmeyer's sedan dangling off the hook, the truck began to weave toward a ditch.

"Watch where you're going," Brassmeyer snapped.

No reply from the driver. They sideswiped an SUV and bashed a headlight against the pickup in front of them.

"Hey, wake up!" the colonel barked.

Tommy looked about in alarm. They weren't the only ones out of control. All around them, vehicles were colliding like bumper cars at a carnival. Up ahead, a taxi plowed into a telephone pole. A school bus struck a truckload of chickens. Cages dropped to the road in a blizzard of feathers; birds scrambled everywhere.

"Has everybody gone crazy?" Brassmeyer bawled.

Tommy caught sight of the dashboard clock. No — not crazy. It was nine, and this had to be part of the big disaster Jax had been talking about.

Oh, no! Did this mean the others had failed?

That was when he saw the cement truck. It was roaring along the wrong side of the road, heading straight for them. The colonel was reaching for the steering wheel, but he couldn't get his arm all the way across the cab.

Desperately, Tommy thought back to the farmhouse. There was a word — some kind of trigger — that would reverse the effects of this! What was it? *Aurora?* No, that was the name of the whole thing —

The cement truck was bearing down on them, close enough for Tommy to see its driver sitting motionless, his hands off the wheel. There was no time left! What was that word? It was impossible to think with Brassmeyer cursing in his ear.

"Dragonfly!" It popped out of him like a champagne cork.

Instantly, the tow truck's driver came back to himself. He grabbed the wheel and swerved just in time to avoid a head-on collision with the cement mixer. They screeched to a halt on the shoulder and sat gasping.

Brassmeyer rolled down his window for air, and that was when they heard it. People, dozens of them, were running out of houses and stores, shouting the same word:

"Dragonfly!"

And the chaos on the road was starting to come under control.

37

The plane hurtled down at them, screaming as it plunged from the sky. The three hypnotists could only watch in awe, imagining the fiery impact. Even if Jax had known that his parents were aboard, his horror could not have been any greater.

"No," Kira barely whispered.

A crash seemed inevitable, mere seconds away. The airliner was so close that Jax could see — or was it a mirage? — the terrified pilot in the cockpit, straining against the controls.

Then, almost by magic, the jet pulled out of its dive, missing the top of the UN by perhaps thirty feet. It climbed, banking over Manhattan.

"That was —" Stanley croaked. He lacked the breath to finish his sentence.

"— close," Jax supplied. His entire body was vibrating at high frequency, like a guitar string.

It wasn't until the plane had turned east toward the airport that the three had a chance to take in the state of the city around them.

The cars packing First Avenue were dented and

smashed, front ends leaking fluids and issuing steam. Hypnotized drivers sat behind deployed airbags. The sidewalks were clogged with pedestrians standing stock-still, and vehicles that had climbed the curb, and bumped into storefronts and poles. Awnings and signs had come down; mailboxes and trash cans had toppled over; plate-glass windows had shattered. Burglar alarms wailed.

A double-decker sightseeing bus drove into the side of a building. Its tires spun and burned rubber as its driver's foot grew heavy on the gas pedal. A few tourists were crying out for rescue, but most sat, impassive. On the East River, a ferry collided with the dock, bounced off, and bobbed there, disabled.

Everywhere, plumes of smoke rose — dozens, no, hundreds of them. To the east — more smoke over Queens and farther out on Long Island.

"Look," mourned Stanley, surveying the chaos.

To Jax, it was eerily familiar. He had seen it happen to tiny Delta Prime in the Arizona desert. Now it was vast New York, and beyond that, the entire planet. Somewhere, all the people he'd ever known must be caught up in this — the soldiers at Fort Calhoun, his classmates in Manhattan and Connecticut, Tommy, Mom, and Dad. But it seemed selfish to dwell on that because *everybody* was caught up in it. No one would escape the chaos that had begun, and understanding what it was or how it worked only made it more horrifying. Jax had heard the projected numbers whispered around HoWaRD after the original Operation Aurora:

how many billions in damage; how many injuries; how many deaths.

The world was about to find out.

"What happens now?" asked Stanley in awe.

Jax did not reply. There was nothing to say. How did you tell an eight-year-old that the end of the world had started — and by his own hand?

At first, the shouting failed to breach the cocoon of Jax's misery. Then Kira elbowed him in the ribs. "Listen!"

The wailing of alarms and sirens was punctuated by the voices of people yelling, whooping, shrieking a single word:

"Dragonfly!"

Once Jax heard it, he realized it was coming from everywhere — windows, doorways, balconies, and rooftops. A fire truck squeezed around the corner, honking its air horn and broadcasting *"Dragonfly!"* over its external speaker. The UN's public-address system burst to life, blasting the word up and down First Avenue. The message was passed from building to building and block to block all around the city.

The three hypnotists watched in astonishment as the thousands of frozen figures stirred and came back to life. Pedestrians moved again. Drivers stepped out of their cars and faced their fender benders. People came down from buildings and flooded the streets. The newly awakened rushed to help the injured. And through it all, the chorus seemed to swell:

"Dragonfly! Dragonfly! Dragonfly!"

Slowly, incredibly, New York City was returning to normal.

"It can't be just here, right?" Kira asked anxiously. "This must be happening everywhere!"

Jax nodded slowly, almost reluctant to jinx this miracle recovery with too much hope. "The command went out to the biggest audience in history."

"We did it!" cheered Stanley.

Jax and Kira both hugged him.

As the effects of the global Aurora began to diminish, police sirens sounded around the city. It was good news, Jax knew. The first responders were recovered enough to do their jobs. Order was about to be restored.

"We should probably get out of here," he decided. "You know, before a few hundred world leaders remember something about kids at the UN."

"Where are we going to go?" asked Stanley, who had left all the family he'd ever known flaked out on the dais of the General Assembly.

"It doesn't matter," Jax replied. "Just away. Right now, that's the only direction we have to worry about. I hope you've got your hiking boots on. It'll be hours before these roads are clear."

Stanley pointed. "We don't have to walk. Look!"

At the base of the flag of Uruguay stood Black Quack, perfectly behaved, waiting patiently.

Moments later, there were reports of one of the stranger sights of that very strange morning — three young people riding through the gridlocked city on a magnificent black thoroughbred.

38

As countries around the globe took stock of the damage caused by the extraordinary events of October 24, the numbers began to mount up. Seven and a half million minor injuries, ranging from cuts and bruises to small burns and broken bones. Eleven million traffic accidents, mostly fender benders.

Remarkably, not a single person was killed.

The world got off easy.

Reports and statistics came from every country, province, city, town, and village. Yet no one had the answer to one very simple question: Why? What had made upward of a billion people suddenly stop dead?

Theories abounded. Astronomers proposed that a large solar flare might have bombarded the earth with photons and affected human minds. Doctors suggested that this was a side effect of fluoride in drinking water. Geophysicists speculated that this might be the first sign of the earth's magnetic poles reversing. The UFO Society concluded it was a mind-control experiment conducted by an alien spacecraft. A group called Ban Technology Now put the blame on "brain hackers" who had found a way to beam a virus directly into people's heads through social media. There was even a cult that believed the millions shouting "Dragonfly!" proved that a giant, all-powerful insect was in charge of the universe.

"Talk about stupid," was Tommy's opinion. "Not one of them said mass hypnotism. It's so obvious!"

"You don't know anything about that," Jax warned. "And you better forget what you do know. No good can ever come from people finding out what really happened."

The two were at I.S. 222, which was the only place they could get together these days. Tommy had been grounded for his twenty-four-hour disappearing act. He tried to convince his parents that he'd been wrapped up in the temporary insanity that had come to be called "The Dragonfly Effect." The Cicerellis weren't buying it.

Jax was happy that the Opuses were in New York again. The aftermath of global chaos wasn't the most convenient time for a cross-country move. But nothing would stop Mom and Dad once they got the green light to start putting their old lives back together again. Monica Opus had already rented an office to restart her chiropractic clinic. Ashton couldn't return to his old job, since everyone at the Bentley dealership had been hypnotized to forget he'd ever worked there. However, Manhattan Bugatti remembered his great reputation as a sales manager and hired him on the spot. Things were finally looking up for Mom and Dad. After all the sacrifices they'd made to protect their son, Jax felt fantastic about that.

What had really made all this possible was the fact that Dr. Mako was no longer a threat to the Opuses or to anybody else. When the police had discovered the identity of the unconscious man at the United Nations, he'd been arrested as an escaped convict. It soon became apparent, though, that this was not the same Elias Mako who'd escaped from a maximum-security prison. The mesmeric attack of the combined powers of Jax and Stanley had left him an empty shell, with very little mind and no memory. He was judged incompetent to go back to jail and sent to live out the rest of his days in a New York nursing home.

Jax and Kira paid him one visit just to prove to themselves that the world was now safe from this man. It was a shock to see him. His black hair was streaked with gray, his expression blank, his eyes vacant. He looked easily thirty years older than before.

He sat in an arts-and-crafts class, rolling a ball of clay between his palms. When Jax and Kira introduced themselves, there was no spark of recognition. His speech was slurred, the commanding voice gone.

"Nice to meet you," he told them.

"Wow," breathed Kira afterward. "I never thought I'd say this, but I actually feel bad for Dr. Mako."

"I don't," Jax said firmly. "Think about what he tried to do — and how close he came to succeeding."

"He said he wanted to use hypnotism to make the world a better place."

"Right," Jax put in sarcastically. "A better place for *him*."

Kira was not convinced. "We can't be sure what his intentions were at the very beginning. He might have started out good, but the power corrupted him. Maybe hypnotism is just too dangerous to be used by anybody."

The United States military seemed to agree. Shortly after the events of October 24, the army shut down its Hypnotic Warfare Research Department on the grounds that mesmeric power was fundamentally unstable. There was no formal announcement. HoWaRD hadn't officially existed in the first place, so it couldn't technically be disbanded.

Colonel Brassmeyer was transferred to a "safer" unit in charge of tracking down loose nukes. Captain Pedroia retired from the army and went into private practice. The psychiatrist and his fiancée were adopting a child — eight-year-old Stanley X, soon to be Stanley Pedroia, an ordinary third grader in Dubuque, Iowa. The military's top computer experts made sure that no one would ever find Stanley's face on an Internet video that had very nearly demolished human civilization.

The army was out of the hypnotism business. None of it had ever happened.

"Would Jackson Opus please report to Principal Orenstein's office."

In the cafeteria, Tommy shot Jax a raised eyebrow. "Still thrilled to be back at school?"

Jax grinned. "I took on Mako. What do I have to fear from Orenstein? A detention? After what I've been through, I'd gladly drop to my knees and kiss the floor of the detention room."

"Easy for you to say," Tommy countered. "All you have to do is bend the guy. Detention? What detention? Straight As? No problem. Student body president? Wouldn't you rather be king?"

"That stops right here," Jax announced sternly. "No more hypnotism. I made a promise to myself and to Axel Braintree's memory that I'm never going to use that power again."

Tommy was unimpressed. "I give you three days. A week, tops."

"I really mean it, Tommy. Evelyn Lolis is back in town and she's starting up the meetings behind the Laundromat."

"You mean that Sandman's Guild?" Tommy asked.

"Well, it's Sand*person*'s Guild now, but it's the same thing. Kira's going with me. We're going to kick the hypnotism habit once and for all."

He bused his tray and made for the main office, taking in his surroundings as if noticing them for the first time. How many long afternoons had he walked these halls, staring from clock to clock, willing the day to hurry up and be over? The place was almost sacred to him now. A *normal* life — how precious was that?

Principal Orenstein was waiting for him with his entire student file spread out across the desk.

"We have a problem here, Jackson, and I can't quite figure it out. You're in eighth grade, but there's no evidence here of you having completed the seventh-grade exams. I know you've been at other schools, but those records should have been forwarded automatically. I can't have an eighth grader who's never finished seventh."

Jax took a deep breath. Even Axel had admitted that controlling the urge to use hypnotism was a matter of one day at a time.

I guess this isn't my day.

He stared at his principal, the irises that had saved the world darkening from green to blue to violet.

"Look into my eyes. . . ."

Gordon Korman is the #1 bestselling author of five books in The 39 Clues series as well as seven books in his Swindle series: *Swindle, Zoobreak, Framed, Showoff, Hideout, Jackpot,* and *Unleashed.* His other books include *This Can't Be Happening at Macdonald Hall!* (published when he was fourteen); *The Toilet Paper Tigers; Radio Fifth Grade; The Chicken Doesn't Skate*; the trilogies Island, Everest, Dive, Kidnapped, and Titanic; and the series On the Run. He lives in New York with his family and can be found on the web at www.gordonkorman.com.